THE GEMINI RISING
ROCKIN' MACHINE

TRIPLE PLAY OF LOVE
SADNESS AND SEXY LUST

Featuring The Triple Play Of Books:
Book Fifteen: Pink Hearts
Book Sixteen: Sexual Amnesia
Book Seventeen: Party In Your Panties

Copyright 2016 by The Gemini Rising Rockin' Machine

**ISBN-13: 978-0692617526 (Gemini Rising Rockin'
Machine,The)**
ISBN-10: 0692617523

For questions, comments you may send correspondence to.

thegeminirisingrockinmachine@twc.com

Official Website
www.thegeminirisingrockinmachine.com

Love And Sadness (Life Is Not Fair) (954.)

You-Know – I-Love-You
The-Smiles – The-Frowns
Love-In-Our-Hearts
Together – We-Stayed
As-The-Years – Passed-By

You-Know – I-Love-You
In-My-Heart – That's-Breaking
I-Have to Say – It's-Not-You
It's-Me – That-Has to End
Our-Love

(Chorus)
Love And Sadness
She Thinks I'm A Dirty Cheater
Love And Sadness
She Thinks I Don't Love Her
Love And Sadness
I Can't Tell Her I'm Dying
Love And Sadness
I Want Her To Be Free
Love And Sadness
Life Is Not Fair

You-Know – I-Love-You
Sorry-My-Love – I've-Changed
Inside-I'm-Dying – When-I-Tell-You
I-Love-Someone-Else
I-Hope-It-Becomes-Heaven – Not-Hell

(Chorus)
Love And Sadness
She Thinks I'm A Dirty Cheater
Love And Sadness
She Thinks I Don't Love Her
Love And Sadness
I Can't Tell Her I'm Dying
Love And Sadness
I Want Her To Be Free
Love And Sadness
Life Is Not Fair

Sexy Lust (Feel The Passion) (955.)

Sexy-Face and Body
Feel-My – Sexy-Lust
Baby-I'm-Ready – For-Some-Lust
That-Never – Slows-Down

Up and Down – Oh-Yeah
Bite-My-Neck as You-Purr
I'll-Pat – Your-Fine-Tail
As-I-Roar and Howl
To-All – The-Sexy-Lust
That-We'll be Sharing

(Chorus)
Sexy Lust – Feel The Passion
Look At Me – Look At You
We Should Be Screwing
Sexy Lust – Feel The Passion
Look At Me – Look At You
We Should Screw All Night
Sexy Lust – Sexy-Lust
Look At Me – Look At You
Your Friend's Hot – Can She
Join In – On Our Screwing

Two-At-One-Time – Oh-Yeah
Damn – The-Two of You – Were-Great
I-Could-Tell – You-Are-Great-Friends
Go-Ahead – Enjoy-The-Other
While-I – Take a Break – Not-Too
Long of One – 'Cause-I'm a Lustful-Man

(Chorus)
Sexy Lust – Feel The Passion
Look At Me – Look At You
We Should Be Screwing
Sexy Lust – Feel The Passion
Look At Me – Look At You
We Should Screw All Night
Sexy Lust – Sexy-Lust
Look At Me – Look At You
Your Friend's Hot – Can She
Join In – On Our Screwing

3

Story One: Blake and Barbara (John)

What Blake planned to say but did not have a chance to was – "Hello, I notice that you are alone and so am I. You've heard this, I've said this before. But beep it, I'm lonely and you're fine, so sweet looking lady what do you say? Would you like to make love with me after I buy you the three D'S – Drinks, Dinner, and Dessert, whatever you want or whatever it will take for you to say yes to me, so I can enjoy your double D'S."

However this is what happened when Blake said, "Hello, I." "Sit down. Never mind. This is not what I ordered, so walk away, then come back to me and do it right this time."

Blake thinks, what the Beep is going on? This is weird but then again it is hot. I think this lady is either a swinger or she thinks she paid for me to come up to her and give her the night she always wanted. I would kick my ass if I ruined this great sexy night without giving it my very best. Think I'll say this.

"Pardon, beautiful. I am a replacement for you. I'll add this, a much better replacement. Here let me sit down so I can give you my full attention. Beautiful sexy lady, I was just told to come here and give you what you paid for. But due to someone stupid, your original date, he took the information sheet with him so for right now I can only guess what you want me to do for and to you. If I understand correctly you paid for the deluxe package. Is that correct? Um sorry I didn't even get your name."

"Barbara." Says Barbara not amused.

"I like that, Beautiful sexy Barbara. Oh what I am going to do for you, Beautiful sexy Barbara. You're so fine I would almost do for you what you want from me for free. But like you know bills are a bitch and my talented body is all I have to survive with and pay them damn bills."

"Well what I want, what is your name anyway?"

"What do you want my name to be Beautiful sexy Barbara?"

Barbara blushes and says, "I don't know."

4

Blake smiles knowing that he has Barbara right where he wants her at the same time he is trying to suppress his excitement because this is the greatest pre-sex thing that has ever happened to him.

"Tell you what Beautiful sexy Barbara, just call me Animal."

"Animal? I think not you bad, bad man. I'll just call you God, like that is what you better make me say over and over again if you know what I mean."

Blake is very turned on when he says, "No that won't do. Barbara you will have to call me God-God because I am twice the special that you can't help but fall in loving love with."

"John, I'm going to call you John for now. John you have turned me on like I have not been in a very long time. Please whatever you do, do not be all about bragging with me and when you get me all alone you are just like everybody else. Give me a little then get yours before I am even half way there.

You see I am divorced, couple of years now, I've had my dates and boy friends but in the end they all turned out the same wanting to be my soon to be lazy man that gives it to me like they and only they want to, which pisses me off John. Like I have no say in it, don't get me started. I'm single, I'm rich, and you better make me moan. Sorry John that Ex of mine still pisses me off so much. I mean look at me I'm hot and he takes off with some young slut that wants to live free in the forest like they did a long time ago. I hope the bastard runs out of food and the only thing around for him to eat are bugs and tree bark."

"Shut up." "Excuse me!" "Barbara I said shut up. I'm on the clock, I am here to turn you on, not to hear you bitch. So that's a penalty, Barbara." "A penalty John!"

"Yes Barbara, so I want you to stand up, come over to me, sit on my lap and give me a kiss like we are the only ones in this entire room."

"I will not John." "If you don't Barbara I'll leave you sitting here wanting to be made to feel like a real woman."

"John, please, I can't. I would be so embarrassed." "Barbara do you know anyone here? Do you come here often?" "No never." "Then what do you care what anyone thinks?

5

As far as they are concerned we might just be a couple in love, or a couple that has had a fight and right here in public we make up like the in love couple we are. You only live once Barbara, sit there and do without or get up and get you some like the woman who is so sure of herself that she is willing to pay someone what she could get for free. Well that is not completely true Barbara, you will never have anyone better than me unless of course you pay for me again."

"John, no one, I mean no one has ever talked to me like this. I like it. You better be all that you say."

"That and even more my sweet, Beautiful, sexy Barbara. All you have to do to set yourself free Barbara is do what I say and I'll make you think and feel like the Sun rises and sets in my pants."

"Alright John, you are in control. I'll give myself to you, but please don't break me. I'm very fragile right now."

"Then you are very lucky Barbara because that is my specialty. Now 1-2-3 come to me my love pet, let me make you feel like you are in Heaven."

Barbara eyes are shining like stars, as her heart is pounding in her chest, she wonders if John can hear her heartbeat as she sits on his lap, giving him the kiss he demanded from her.

Waiter comes to John and Barbara's table saying, "Please, please we cannot have that in here, this is a respectable, first class restaurant."

John says, "Well then shut up and bring us your best bottle of champagne and don't forget this fine lady is going to pay for everything."

Barbara gets off of John's lap, the waiter looks jealously at his table guests then walks away doing what he was commanded to do. Dinner is over, John and Barbara go to a hotel for a second helping of dessert.

Blake pulls no kisses as he makes sure to give Barbara everything she always wanted. All is well and fine as Blake starts to think too much about doing the right thing.

"Barbara my name is Blake and I am not who you think I am." "You're not?" "No I am not.

I am just a lonely man that came up to you for a chance of having a great time. I am not the man you ordered or even the man that took his place."

"What!? This can not be. You bastard! What kind of man are you, to do this to me? I hope you had your fun because I am going to destroy you, you bastard."

"Barbara please wait a minute. At first yes, my only intention was to use you for a great time but now Barbara, I love you."

"Love me!? Love me!? I don't even know who you are. I can't believe this I feel sick, I think I should go to the hospital."

"Now wait a minute Barbara, it's not like I have a disease or something. And to be honest, you are not so innocent Barbara. You did after all pay someone to make love to you or should I say to have sex with you."

"That is true, I paid for one of them and you are not one of them. You're just normal, not special. I just knew it, deep down I knew something was going on, you were good but not great."

"Well I know my ears are ringing from your loud lustful moaning in them. You were really loud, deny it all you want, I know you enjoyed me lots while I just had a good time."

"Well Blake let's see how good of a time you have when I call the cops and tell them how you took advantage of me all for money. I'll tell them I was weak and all that. How does that sound to you Blake? Does that sound Jake to you? Ha,ha, ha."

"Sounds like a bunch of shit to me, you Witch." "Say you're sorry or I'll call right now!" "I'm Sorry! You." "You what?" "You very pretty lady."

"That's better, maybe I have a use for you after all. Okay this is the way it is going to be. You come when I call you. You don't ever tell anyone and maybe just maybe, I'll let you be my love toy. Just nod your head yes. That's a good love pet, now get the Hell out of here I'm done with you for now." Blake leaves. Barbara thinks to herself, " Men are so easy and dumb."

7

Book Fifteen: Pink Hearts (Pages 8-30)

(Side One)
281. Pink Hearts (761.)
282. Lemon Yellow Sun / Lime Green Grass (762.)
283. Can You Feel My Heart (737.)
284. Gray Skies And Smiles (763.)
285. At First Sight (764.)

(Side Two)
286. Peace Of Mind (765.)
287. Love Has A Mind Of Its Own (766.)
288. To Be Your Happy Man (767.)
289. The Sweet Scent Of Love (768.)
290. Do You Care (770.)

(Side Three)
291. Easy Lover (771.)
292. Give Me One More Time (772.)
293. Love Yourself (773.)
294. The Road Of Love (774.) (New Name)
295. Love Party Of Two (775.)

(Side Four)
296. Happiness With Sadness (776.) (New Name)
297. Here's My Heart (778.)
298. Can You Love Me (780.)
299. Love Fever (781.)
300. Best Of Everything (782.)

(Bonus Songs)
You're In Love (No Way To Fight It) (783.)
I Love You Baby (Do You Love Me) (784.)

281. Pink Hearts

(Pink – Her)
Hearts of Pink – Tell-Me – What-You-Think
Blue-Skies – With-Balloons of Red
Filled-With-Love is All-In-My-Head
Tell-Me is This-Love – I-Feel
Really and Truly for Real

(Hearts – Him)
You and Me – Forever
Brightness in Your-Eyes
Flush of Our-Love – All-Over
Your-Pretty-Face – Makes-Me-Sing

(Chorus – Pink Hearts)
Pink Hearts Filled With Love
Brings The End – To Our Loneliness
Pink Hearts Filled With Love
Realigns Two Separate Hearts
Pink Hearts Filled With Love
Proves Love – Is The Best Thing On Earth

(Pink – Her)
I'm so Happy – You're-Mine
Not a Day – Goes by That-I
Don't-Look at You and Sigh
Feeling-Our – Hearts of Pink

(Hearts – Him)
Yes-I-Know – I'm-Lucky
To-Love a Lady – Like-You
Happy-Baby – You-Feel the Same
Come on Baby – Let's-Sing-Our-Song
Let's-Show-The-World – Our-Hearts of Pink

(Chorus – Pink Hearts)
Pink Hearts Filled With Love
Brings The End – To Our Loneliness
Pink Hearts Filled With Love
Realigns Two Separate Hearts
Pink Hearts Filled With Love
Proves Love – Is The Best Thing On Earth

282. Lemon Yellow Sun / Lime Green Grass

Lemon Yellow Sun

Happy on My-Face
Love in My-Heart
I'm-Dancing to Nowhere – and
Loving – Every-Minute of It

Mother-Earth is So-Beautiful
Just-Like-The-One – That-I-Love
Time is Ticking-Away – So-Slowly
Can't-Wait to Kiss-Her Deeply

(Chorus)
Lemon Yellow Sun
In The Blue Sky
Guide My Love To Me
Lemon Yellow Sun
Thank You For Your Warmth
Lemon Yellow Sun
Shine Down On Me Forever
(Repeat All)

Lime Green Grass

My-Love – There-She is Now
Walking – Barefoot-Along
In-The-Lime – Green-Grass
Her-Smile – I-Can-See-From-Here
Just-Like-I – She-Can't-Wait to Feel-Me

She-Stops-Walking as The-Wind-Blows
Its-Sweet-Summer-Scent
Making-The-Love – She-Feels-For-Me
Blossom-Even – Stronger-In-Her-Heart

(Chorus)
Stay Where You Are My Love
Let's Make Slow Loving Love
In The Lime Green Grass
While The Lemon Yellow Sun
Shines Down – Warm Upon Us
(Repeat All)

283. Can You Feel My Heart

Love-For-You – Beats-In-My-Heart
Your-Face – Always on My-Mind
Yesterday – Today – Tomorrow
I-Hope-This – Never-Changes – One-Bit
Because-Baby – I-Love-You

(Chorus)
Can You Feel – Can You Feel My Heart
It Beats Just For You
Can You Feel – Can You Feel My Heart
Let's Honeymoon On A Beach
Can You Feel – Can You Feel My Heart
It's Yours Baby – It's Yours Baby
Don't Play With It – Just Love It Lots And Lots

Did I Mention – That It Comes – With A Lifetime Of Love

Rain – Cold – They-Don't-Matter
When-We-Feel – Love and Sunshine
Our-Hearts – Have-Become-One
Let's-Not – Waste a Moment
Please-Become – My-Wife

(Chorus)
Can You Feel – Can You Feel My Heart
It Beats Just For You
Can You Feel – Can You Feel My Heart
Let's Honeymoon On A Beach
Can You Feel – Can You Feel My Heart
It's Yours Baby – It's Yours Baby
Don't Play With It – Just Love It Lots And Lots

Did I Mention – That It Comes – With A Lifetime Of Love

One-Year – Turns to Ten
Ten-Years – Turns to Twenty
Still-Love-For-You – Beats in My-Heart
Like a Slow – Walk in The-Park
Making-Me-Feel – So-Glad to Be-Alive

(Repeat Chorus)

284. Gray Skies And Smiles

Raining it's Raining and I-Love-You
Say it With-Me-Baby
That-You – Love-Me-Too – Oh-Darling
I-Know – That-You-Do
Which-Makes – My-Love-For-You
Rise-Up-Lovely – Inside-My-Heart

Gray-Skies-Today – My-Love
That-Don't – Worry-Me-Much
'Cause – We're on The-Couch
Having a Great-Time

(Chorus)
Gray Skies And Smiles
On This Rainy Day In May
We Love To Hang Out And Talk
Having A Great Time
Knowing We Love The Other
That Makes These Gray Skies
Seem As Blue As They Can Be

Hey-Baby – I-Know it's Raining
But-I-Feel – Wild and Free
Baby-Let's-Go – Out in The-Rain
'Cause-Baby – I-Feel-Dirty

Baby – Let's-Wash-The-World – Off-Us
It's-Not – Our-Fault – We're-Dirty
Let's-Rinse-All – The-Funk-Off
Then-Go-Back and Sit on The-Couch
Maybe-We-Can – Kiss a Little-Bit
That-I-Won't-Mind – One-Little-Bit

(Chorus)
Gray Skies And Smiles
On This Rainy Day In May
We Love To Hang Out And Talk
Having A Great Time
Knowing We Love The Other
That Makes These Gray Skies
Seem As Blue As They Can Be

12

285. At First Sight

Hello-Beautiful
Can-You – Do-Something-For-Me
I-Like-My-Coffee – With-No-Sweetness
Yet-Today – I'd-Like a Little-Sweetness

If-You-Would – Please-Take a Drink
I-Know – That-Would – Sweeten-It
Just so Perfectly – Can-You
Help-Me-Out – Beautiful

(Chorus)
I Fell In Love With You
At First Sight
Watching You Drink My Coffee
Laughing And Spilling Some
You Are So Beautiful Baby
First Sight – Every Sight After That

Looking at You – From-Afar
You're so Beautiful – You've-Heard it All-Before
Cup of Coffee – In-My-Hand
Ready to Fall – In-Love
Walking-Over to Make-You-Smile
Knowing – Just-What to Say

Hello-Beautiful
Can-You – Do-Something-For-Me
I-Like-My-Coffee – With-No-Sweetness
Yet-Today – I'd-Like a Little-Sweetness

If-You-Would – Please-Take a Drink
I-Know – That-Would – Sweeten-It
Just so Perfectly – Can-You
Help-Me-Out – Beautiful

(Chorus)
I Fell In Love With You
At First Sight – Baby
Watching You Drink My Coffee
Laughing And Spilling Some
You Are So Beautiful Baby
First Sight – Every Sight After That

13

286. Peace Of Mind

You-Never – Can-Tell – Can-You
Will-Love-Stay – Will-It-End
One-Day – You're-Happy
One-Day – You're-Sad
Love-Has a Mind of Its-Own

Day to Day – Is-How-I – Took-It
Falling-In and Falling-Out of Love
Until-I – Met-You
When-Your-Love – Gave-Me-A

(Chorus)
Peace Of Mind
That's What I Have
Peace Of Mind
All Because Of You
Peace Of Mind
Because You Love Me
And I Love You

Heart in My-Hands – Ready for Anything
There-You-Were – Looking-Alone
What-Could-I-Do – But-Try

We-Kissed – My-Heart – Slowed-Down
Magic-Lit – The-Sky-Up – With-Desire
World-Stopped-Spinning
While-We-Made-Love – For-The First-Time

When-We – Were Done – You-Said
Baby – I-Love-You
Giving-Me a Forever

(Chorus)
Peace Of Mind
That's What I Have
Peace Of Mind
All Because Of You
Peace Of Mind
Because You Love Me
And I Love You

287. Love Has A Mind Of Its Own

Good-Love – Bad-Love
They-Come and They-Go
I-Say – Love-It
Better-Than-Being – All-Alone

Afternoon – Brunch-Delight
Dinner-Time – Love-Match
Love-Can-Stay – Far-Behind-You
Love-Can – Come-Up to You and
Hit-You – Right-Between-The-Eyes
All-I-Know is That

(Chorus)
Love Has A Mind Of Its Own
What Can You Do – But Say
Love Has A Mind Of Its Own
It Is The Way That It Is
Love Has A Mind Of Its Own
That's Why – It Lights You Up
That's Why – It Breaks Your Heart
Love Has A Mind Of Its Own
Would You Really Want This To Change

First-Kiss – Last-Kiss
Did-She – Kiss-Me-Goodbye –Last-Night
Will-I-find – Someone-New to Kiss – Tonight
Will-I-Be – All by Myself
Looking for Love – Not-Finding-It
Don't-Know – All-I-Know is That

(Chorus)
Love Has A Mind Of Its Own
What Can You Do – But Say
Love Has A Mind Of Its Own
It Is The Way That It Is
Love Has A Mind Of Its Own
That's Why – It Lights You Up
That's Why – It Breaks Your Heart
Love Has A Mind Of Its Own
Would You Really Want This To Change

288. To Be Your Happy Man

We-Walk – Across-The-Desert
Without a Drop of Water to Drink
We-Fly – High in The-Sky
Without-Wings to Spread-Free

Still-I'm-Happy to Be-Your-Man
Darling-You-Mean – Everything to Me
Forever-I-Will-Be – Your-Man
All-You-Have to Do-Is – Give-Me a Kiss
I-Will-Be – So-Happy

(Chorus)
To Be Your Happy Man
Yes That's Right – Yes That's True
I'm Your Happy Man – Baby
Feel My Heartbeat – Look Into My Eyes
I Will Always Love – To Be Your Happy Man

We-Sail – Across-The-River
Our-Ship – Springs a Leak
We-Make-Love so Wonderfully
Candles – Get-Knocked-Over
Room-Catches on Fire
While-We-Try – Catching-Our-Breath

Still-I'm-Happy to Be-Your-Man
Darling-You-Mean – Everything to Me
Forever-I-Will-Be – Your-Man
All-You-Have to Do-Is – Give-Me a Kiss
I-Will-Be – So-Happy

(Chorus)
To Be Your Happy Man
Yes That's Right – Yes That's True
I'm Your Happy Man – Baby
Feel My Heartbeat – Look Into My Eyes
I Will Always Love – To Be Your Happy Man

289. The Sweet Scent Of Love

I-Hear – The-Love-Bell – Ringing
Inside-My – Lonely by Myself – Heart
I-Get-Up and Get-My-Loveless
Body-Up and Out to Search for Love

Searched for Love – Yesterday
Searching for Love – Today
My-Soul – Feels so Heavy – What-Can-I-Do
Will-Love-Find-Me – Wait a Minute – What is That
Sweet and Loving – Scent-In-The-Air

(Chorus)
I Can Smell It – I Can Smell It
The Sweet Scent Of Love
Flowing – Lovingly In The Air
I Won't Let It Pass Me By This Time
I Will Inhale – I Will Inhale
All-That Sweet Scent Of Love – All Up
Having Love – Finally Enlighten Me
To The Point – That I Will Be Loved Forever

I-Hear – The-Love-Bell – Ringing
Inside-My – Lonely by Myself – Heart
I-Get-Up and Get-My-Loveless
Body-Up and Out to Search for Love

Searched for Love – Yesterday
Searching for Love – Today
My-Soul – Feels so Heavy – What-Can-I-Do
Will-Love-Find-Me – Wait a Minute – What is That
Sweet and Loving – Scent-In-The-Air

(Chorus)
I Can Smell It – I Can Smell It
The Sweet Scent Of Love
Flowing – Lovingly In The Air
I Won't Let It Pass Me By This Time
I Will Inhale – I Will Inhale
All-That Sweet Scent Of Love – All Up
Having Love – Finally Enlighten Me
To The Point – That I Will Be Loved Forever

290. Do You Care

I-Ask-Myself – Why-Why-Why
Can't-You – Just-Love-Me
Do-I – Still-Turn-You-On
Have-I-Been – Turning-You-Off
I-Just-Don't-Know – Baby
I-Do-Know – That-I – Miss-You so Much

I-Ask-Myself – Where-Has-She-Gone
While-I – Ask-You-This-Baby

(Chorus)
Do You Care – That I'm Lonely
Do You Care – That I Need You
Do You Care – That I Love You
Do You Care – About Anything Baby
Do You Care – That I'm Lonely
Do You Care – That I Need You
Do You Care – That I Love You
Do You Care – About Anything Baby

Just-Tell-Me-Baby
Better to Let it All-Out
Than to Let-It – Harden-Your-Heart
For-Once – Upon a Time – Your-Smile
Could-Stop-Time – Making
My-Heart – Beat-Out of My-Chest
From-The-Burning-Love – That-Was-You

I-Ask-Myself – Where-Has-She-Gone
While-I – Ask-You-This-Baby

(Chorus)
Do You Care – That I'm Lonely
Do You Care – That I Need You
Do You Care – That I Love You
Do You Care – About Anything Baby
Do You Care – That I'm Lonely
Do You Care – That I Need You
Do You Care – That I Love You
Do You Care – About Anything Baby

291. Easy Lover

I-Was-In-Love – Got-My-Heartbroken
Stayed by Myself – Healing-My-Pains
Rock and Rolling – The-Night-Away
Like-The-Pain – Was-Already-Gone

You-Know-Me – I-Know-You
We-Say-Hello – How-Have-You-Been
When-We – Bump-Into-Each-Other
One-Out of Every – Thirty-Days
Then-You-Kissed-Me – Making-My-Heart-Thump

(Chorus)
You're Such An Easy Lover
Your Love Feels So Fine
Making My Heart – Beat Faster And Faster
Oh Baby – Oh Baby
Can't Believe My Luck
To Find An Easy Lover Like You
That Wants To Love-Me – Instead Of Breaking-My-Heart

We-Kissed – I-Pulled-Away
You-Cried – Saying-You're – Not-Them
I-Have to Believe – In-Your-Love
If-I-Ever-Want to Get
Out of My-Love-Slump
On to The-Wonder – That is Love

You-Know-Me – I-Know-You
We-Are in Love – With-Each-Other
You -Kissed-Me and Kissed-Me
Keeping-My-Heart – Beating to Love
Baby-Let's – Dance and Dance

(Chorus)
You're Such An Easy Lover
Your Love Feels So Fine
Making My Heart – Beat Faster And Faster
Oh Baby – Oh Baby
Can't Believe My Luck
To Find An Easy Lover Like You
That Wants To Love-Me – Instead Of Breaking-My-Heart

292. Give Me One More Time

I-Broke – Your-Heart in Two
Having-The-Time of My-Life
Before-I – Could-Stop-Myself
I-Was-Miles – Away-From-You
Looking to Find – My-Way-Back

Here-I am Baby – I'm-Sorry-I
Broke-Your-Heart – Tell-You-What-Baby

(Chorus)
Give Me One More Time
To Prove I'm Not Selfish
Give Me One More Time – Baby
To Prove That I Love You
Give Me One More Time
To Earn Your Faith In Me
Give Me One More Time – Baby
To Feel Your Love Again

Tears in Your-Eyes – You-Forgive-Me
Telling-Me – No-More – This is It – Last-Time
You-Won't-Let-Me – Break-Your-Heart-Again

Wiping-My-Brow – Knowing-How-Close
I-Came to Losing – You-Forever
Wondering-If – I-Should – Toss-My-Black-Book
I-Put it Back – In-My-Pocket – Saying to You

Here-I am Baby – I'm-Sorry-I-Broke
Your-Heart – Tell-You-What-Baby

(Chorus)
Give Me One More Time
To Prove I'm Not Selfish
Give Me One More Time – Baby
To Prove That I Love You
Give Me One More Time
To Earn Your Faith In Me
Give Me One More Time – Baby
To Feel Your Love Again

293. Love Yourself

You-Won't – Talk to Me
I-Bring – You-Flowers
You-Throw – Them-Away
You-Won't – Talk to Me
I-Bring – You-Chocolates
You-Tell-Me to Eat-Them

Because – You're-Not in The-Mood
To-Fall in Love-Today
Even-With-Someone – You-Use to Love

(Chorus)
I Don't Think It's Me
I'm a Great Guy – A Great Catch
I Think It's You Baby
You're So Beautiful To Look At
But Baby I Think This For Sure
If You Want To Feel Some Love
You Need To Learn To Love Yourself First

You-Won't – Talk to Me
Keep-Hanging-Up on Me
You-Won't – Talk to Me
Keep on Closing – The-Door in My-Face
You-Won't – Talk to Me
That's a Shame – Baby
'Cause-You-Need – Someone to Love

Think-I'll-Try – One-More-Time
To-Get – Through to You – Baby
After-This – I-Think – I-Better-Get
Cruising-Along – On-The-Road of Love

(Chorus)
I Don't Think It's Me
I'm a Great Guy – A Great Catch
I Think It's You Baby
You're So Beautiful To Look At
But Baby I Think This For Sure
If You Want To Feel Some Love
You Need To Learn To Love Yourself First

21

294. The Road Of Love

I've-Been on The-Road of Love
For so Long – It's-Hard to Remember
Sometimes-That-I'm – Still-Looking for Love
When-Love-Blocks – Keeps-Me-Guessing
If-This is Love – When-I-Finally – Find-It
Hard to Tell – With a Heart – Inside-Me
That is Very-Soft and Very-Hard – From-The
Constant-Changing-Emotions – That I-Feel

(Chorus)
On The Road Of Love
Lies Good-Good Times
On The Road Of Love
Lays Bad-Times In The Making
On The Road Of Love Sometimes
You Know Just What To Do
On The Road Of Love Sometimes
You Make The Mistake Of Your Life
On The Road Of Love
You Can Give In Or Keep Rolling On

I've-Been on The-Road of Love
For so Long – It's-Hard to Remember
Sometimes-That-I'm – Still-Looking for Love
When-Love-Blocks – Keeps-Me-Guessing
If-This is Love – When-I-Finally – Find-It
Hard to Tell – With a Heart – Inside-Me
That is Very-Soft and Very-Hard – From-The
Constant-Changing-Emotions – That I-Feel

(Chorus)
On The Road Of Love
Lies Good-Good Times
On The Road Of Love
Lays Bad-Times In The Making
On The Road Of Love Sometimes
You Know Just What To Do
On The Road Of Love Sometimes
You Make The Mistake Of Your Life
On The Road Of Love
You Can Give In Or Keep Rolling On

22

295. Love Party Of Two

He-Says-Yes – She-Says-No
She-Says-Yes – He-Says-No
Over and Over and Over
It's-Their-Routine – They-Play so Well
Night-Time is Sleep-Time
Making-Love – Has-Been-Forgotten

Now-Sadly – Their-Love – Is on The-Line
Do-They – Stand a Chance – At a Re-Loving
Will-They – Rip-Their-Love – Apart at The-Seams

(Chorus)
Calling Calling – For A Love Party Of Two
What Is Your Two's Problems
Calling Calling – For A Love Party Of Two
Do You Love The Other – Do You Want To Make Love
Do You Want To Be – Sad And Alone Together
Calling Calling – For A Love Party Of Two
It's Time For Love – Is It Time To Split-Up

He-Says-Yes – She-Says-Maybe
He-Sits-Back in His-Chair
She-Sits on His-Lap – Kissing-Him-Fine
Talking – Messes it All-Up
Once-Again – It's-Back to
Yes and No – No and Yes
With-No-Maybes – Around-For-Pleasures
That-These-Two – Need so Badly

Now-Sadly – Their-Love – Is on The-Line
Do-They – Stand a Chance – At a Re-Loving
Will-They – Rip-Their-Love – Apart at The-Seams

(Chorus)
Calling Calling – For A Love Party Of Two
What Is Your Two's Problems
Calling Calling – For A Love Party Of Two
Do You Love The Other – Do You Want To Make Love
Do You Want To Be – Sad And Alone Together
Calling Calling – For A Love Party Of Two
It's Time For Love – It's Time To Split-Up

296. Happiness With Sadness

Life is Great – When-You're in Love
You-Get to Feel – The Happiness-You-Need
Then-Out-Of a Nightmare – There is Sadness
Lurking-With-Its – Un-Love-In-The-Waiting

Quickly-Taking-Your-Love – Away-From-You
Leaving-You – Empty and Broken
With a Hurting-Heart – With-No-Smile
On-Your-Face to Show-The-Sun

(Chorus)
Happiness With Sadness
This Your Love Life
Happiness With Sadness
You're In Love – You Get Dumped
Happiness With Sadness
Makes Your Love Rise So Rock High
Then It Sinks To Rock Love Bottom

You-Show-Your – Face to The-World
With-Dried – Tears in Your-Eyes
So-Big-This-World – It-Can-Crush-You
Lurking-With-Its – Un-Love-In-The-Waiting

Making-You – Want to Put-On a Mask
So-The-World – Can't-See-Your-Love-Scars
Of-Giving-Your-Heart – Over to Love
Just-In-Case – There-Is a Replay-Of
Every-Lover – You've-Ever-Had – In-Your-Eyes

(Chorus)
Happiness With Sadness
This Your Love Life
Happiness With Sadness
You're In Love – You Get Dumped
Happiness With Sadness
Makes Your Love Rise So Rock High
Then It Sinks To Rock Love Bottom

297. Here's My Heart

Stranded-Alone on My-Island
Deep in The-Middle of My-City
Where-Thousands of Strangers
Live-With-Me – Without-Noticing-Me

I-Live-My-Life – All by Myself
With-No-Love – Coming to My-Shores
Comforting-My-Lonely – Scarred-Heart
That-Wants to Feel – The-Passion-That is Love
With-Love-World – I-Love-This-Out to You

(Chorus)
Here's My Heart
It's Hardly Been Used
Here's My Heart
It's All I Have In This World
Here's My Heart
Try Not To Break It
Here's My Heart
Give It Back – If You Don't Want It

When-You-Go-Away – Why-Do-You
Have to Step on My-Heart
Is it Fun – Is it Exciting
World-Have-You – Grown so Cold

I-Can't-Believe – I-Won't-Believe-That
Love is Stronger – Than-Hate
Love-Makes – This-World-Go-Around
Even if This-World – Doesn't-Believe-It
With-Love-World – I-Love-This-Out to You

(Chorus)
Here's My Heart
It's Hardly Been Used
Here's My Heart
It's All I Have In This World
Here's My Heart
Try Not To Break It
Here's My Heart
Give It Back – If You Don't Want It

25

298. Can You Love Me

I'm-Doing-Fine – With-My-Lover
She's-Kinda a Little – Just-Right
Almost – But-Not-Perfect – Like-I-Need

Is it Me – Is it Her – Hard to Say
All-I-Know Is – I-Got-This-Itch
Starting-Up – Inside-My-Heart

What-Can-I-Do – But-Come-Up to You
And-Say – Hey-Baby

(Chorus)
Can You Love Me – Can You Love Me
If You Got Nothing Better To Do
'Cause I'm Looking For A New Lover
That Will Light My Love And Soul On Fire
Can You Love Me – Can You Love Me
Even If It's Only Make Believe
Even If It Only Lasts A Few Hours

You-Ask if I'm-Love-Crazy
I-Show-You – My-Hairy-Chest
You-Ask if I'm-Love-Crazy
I-Take-Your-Hand and Kiss-Your-Cheek
You-Ask if I'm-Love-Crazy
I-Get-Down on My-Knees

You-Say – Crazy-Enough-For-Me
While-I-Say to You – Hey-Baby

(Chorus)
Can You Love Me – Can You Love Me
If You Got Nothing Better To Do
'Cause I'm Looking For A New Lover
That Will Light My Love And Soul On Fire
Can You Love Me – Can You Love Me
Even If It's Only Make Believe
Even If It Only Lasts A Few Hours

299. Love Fever

Stayed-Up-Late – With-My-Date
She-Was-Cool – And-Fine
I-Almost – Lost-My-Mind
We-Kissed – We-Got-It-On
Great-Day – In-My-Life

Tomorrow-Turned – Into-More of The-Same
As-We-Got-It-On – For-Over 30 Days
I-Was-Sexy-Happy – In-Love
While-She – Played-In-Love
Just to Burn-Me – With-Pride
Loving-The-Look – In-My-Eyes
As-She-Tells-Me – That's-It

Can't-Take-It – Can't-Take-It
Can't-Take-It – Anymore
This is What – My-Love-Has-Become

(Chorus)
Love Fever – Love Fever
Has Got A Hold Of Me
Love Fever – Love Fever
Makes My Soul – Shake With Chills
Love Fever – Love Fever
The-Joy-Pain – From Being In Love
Love Fever – Love Fever
There Is No Cure – For My Heart
Love Fever – Love Fever
Have To Let It Burn Itself Out

I-Might be Burning-Up – In-Regret
But-Yesterday – Was-Such a Pleasure
To-My-Lonely and Burning-Heart
I'm-Still-Willing to Take-My-Chance
That-My-Next-Love – Will-Not-Give-Me
Love Fever – To-Suffer-Through

Can't-Take-It – Can't-Take-It
Can't-Take-It – Anymore
This is What – My-Love-Has-Become

(Repeat Chorus)
27

300. Best Of Everything

Check-This-Out – Everybody
I-Got-It – Going-On
This-Lovely – Lovely-Lady
Asked-Me – If-I-Had-The-Time
I-Told-Her – 10:39
She-Laughed and Said – This to Me

(Chorus)
No-No-No – Stranger
That I Think Is So Sexy-Hot
You Might Not Know This – But
I've Got The Best Of Everything
So What Do You Say Stranger
Do You Want To Have A Great Time
With My Sexy Sweet – Best Of Everything

Check-This-Out – Everybody
My-Life is Like a Love-Fantasy
That's-Come to Life – Better-Than-I
Could-Ever-Dream – For-It to Come to Life
Universe – Must-Be on My-Side
About – Loving-Time

Must-Have – Done-Something – Real-Great
To be Getting – The-Kinda-Love – I'm-Receiving
Check-This-Out-Everybody – Still-Going-Through
My-Mind is Her-Saying – This to Me

(Chorus)
No-No-No – Stranger
That I Think Is So Sexy-Hot
You Might Not Know This – But
I've Got The Best Of Everything
So What Do You Say Stranger
Do You Want To Have A Great Time
With My Sexy Sweet – Best Of Everything

Check-This-Out-Everybody – I-Gotta-Take-Off
It's-10:39 and You-Know – What-I'm-About to Do

(Bonus Song)

You're In Love (No Way To Fight It) (783.)

There-She-Is – All-The-Time
Tempting-You – With-Her-Fineness
You-Try to Look – The-Other-Way
Deep-Down – You-Know – You're-Just
Wasting-Your-Time – You're-Hooked
She's-Got a Hold of Your-Line

(Chorus)
You're In Love – No Way To Fight It
You Can Try And You Can Try
But There Is Nothing You Can Do
You're In Love – No Way To Fight It
Better Just To Give Up – Relax
Letting Love Lighten Your Soul

You-Walk-Away so Slowly
She-Calls-Out to You – Come-Back
You-Come-Running – Wanting-More and More
She-Says-Quicker – You-Follow-Her-Blindly
Face-it-Man-You're-Just – Wasting-Your-Time
You're-Hooked – She's-Got a Hold of Your-Line

(Chorus)
You're In Love – No Way To Fight It
You Can Try And You Can Try
But There Is Nothing You Can Do
You're In Love – No Way To Fight It
Better Just To Give Up – Relax
Letting Love Lighten Your Soul

Calm-Down-Man – She's a Fine-Lady
She's-Been-Hurt-Before – She's-Just
Wondering – What's on Your-Mind
If-You-Truly – Truly-Love-Her
Until-Then – She'll-Play-With-Your-Heart
Face-it-Man-You're-Just – Wasting-Your-Time
You're-Hooked – She's-Got a Hold of Your-Line

(Repeat Chorus)

I Love You Baby (Do You Love Me) (784.)

I-Was-Lost – You-Were-Lost
Love-Was-Not – My-Friend
As-I-Kissed-You – Good-Night

Couple-Days-Later – You-Came-Into-My-Mind
Gave-You a Call – You-Told-Me to Come-Over
Things-Changed-Fast – With-No-Goodbye-Kiss
Turned-Into a Good-Morning-Kiss

(Chorus)
I Love You Baby – Do You Love Me
I Need You Baby – Do You Need Me
The Reason I'm Asking This Baby
Is I Want To Make Sure
Before You Become My – Forever Lover
Instead Of Just Another – One Time Lover
Tell-Me-Baby – Tell-Me-Baby – I-Just-Have to Know

I-Was-Lost – You-Were-Lost
Love-Was-Not – My-Friend
Until-I-Met-You – Baby

Changes-Galore – Happened to My-Heart
Fast-Very-Fast – Made-My-Knees go All-Weak
Love – I-Felt it Before – But-Not-Like-This

I-Look Into-My-Heart and Ask-It
If-You-Are – The-One-For-Me
Then-I-Look at You and Say

(Chorus)
I Love You Baby – Do You Love Me
I Need You Baby – Do You Need Me
The Reason – I'm Asking This Baby
Is I Want To Make Sure
Before You Become My – Forever Lover
Instead Of Just – Another One Time Lover
Tell-Me-Baby – Tell-Me-Baby – I-Just-Have to Know

Story Two: Jim and Jill

"Wake up, please wake up Paul. They're coming Paul, they look so pissed off, wake up damn it. I need some help. Okay you got us, no need in going crazy. We were just having fun, no one got hurt, except my man here. You didn't have to shoot him. Please just let us go he needs a doctor."

Bad guys walk closer, looking at their good looking prisoner, enjoying that her man is dying. Unnamed Blonde waits so patiently, then says, "Fools take this." Unnamed Blonde pulls out her pistol and like the great assassin she is, she blows all five of them away with such ease it is almost as beautiful as she is.

"Paul oh Paul, I did it, I love you so much. In your dreams you stupid tool. Fool take this." Unnamed Blonde raises her pistol and like the great assassin she is, she gives Paul the fool in love his fast, cold death.

"Cut! That's a wrap. Jill you were great."

"Thanks Jim. I feel so great, that scene went so great this time. I just love this character, she is so sexy-bad-ass with her gun. Jim I feel so positive that this movie will be my big break. Thank you Jim for giving me this chance."

"Jill you were born for this role, I should be thanking you for gracing us with your performance."

After scene talking continues for around thirty minutes, Jim and Jill can't wait to be alone. (30 + 10 minutes later, in a trailer.)

"Jim make love to me like I deserve, like the star I am. Jim I love you this is so great, I just love our secret. We get to have as much fun as we want and nobody but us knows any different. It makes me laugh, Jim, that to everyone else we are just good friends and you are so much in love with that not good enough for you girlfriend of yours. Damn it Jim every time I feel so great that bitch has to come to my mind and ruin my mood. I just don't know how much more of that bitch I can take. Why can't you drop her? She's not famous, she's not a star like I am."

"Jill my love, you know quite well, because I tell you all the time. She's money, lots of it, just enjoy the fact my love, that we are getting ready to make love in a trailer,

31

filled with roses, champagne, and great food all paid in full by her. Now tell me, Jill my love what in the whole wide world could be better than this?"

"Damn it, alright alright, yes I love spending her money. Now let me up, I want to put on my fur coat so you can make love to me while I'm wearing it."

"Fine but first grab me a beer this champagne sucks." "How romantic, but you have to drink it first and fast. I'm getting tired and I don't want you to spill any of your damn beer on my beautiful fur coat."

"Oh yes my dear starlet of mine. And just because you are so special, I'll even pop in a breath mint just so you won't have to taste beer on my breath while we're getting it on."

"Getting it on? Really!? I do not get it on Jim, I make love. Damn it. That's it you just fudged up the night. You ungrateful man, I don't know why I put up with you."

"Put up with me? Jill you are a twit."

"What? How dare you? I'll let you know this. I am the star, baby. That's right, get use to it, baby. Because without me this movie and you would be nothing. Now get out of my trailer, you ungrateful man, you."

"If I get out Jill, you're out on your pretty ass with no fur coat. Then so sad, I would have to tell all about how difficult you are to work with. Even worse, how you tried to seduce me. A man like me that is like a rock when it comes to having sex with anyone but my love."

"Jim you are a bastard." "And Jill you are a bitch, and so what. We're great I tell you. Now let's forget all this extra heavy and make love like only two shining stars like us can make."

"Damn Jim, what can I say? Sometimes I forget how good I got it. Still you are a bastard and for right now I like that, come and get me, Mr. Director, fur coat and all."

Jim and Jill make love, each believing that they are the more special one in this sexy Hollywood relationship. The next day, Jim is talking to someone on the phone, that is not well known in Hollywood but feared, just like all those that are like him in Hollywood.

This person is the dirt stirrer. This person can make or destroy a career.

Jim on the phone, "She has had her turn, sadly just like all the others she thought she could pull off that Me, me, me routine. So since she blew it and not in the correct way all I can say to her, is so sad, baby.

So this is the way I want it, we should be done filming in five days but since she thinks she is a superstar better make that in seven days. On this seventh day, our very heartwarming final day of shooting and the last time we do it, Ha. I want her splashed everywhere with some nasty that makes her look nasty and not worth wanting anymore. I don't want her to feel even one minute of her fifteen moments of fame. Which will lead us so pretty to my second thing I want you to do for me.

Time to strike close to home. Who am I kidding? Right in the dead center of my home is where I will strike. My bride to be will feel the strain deeply from the financial loss of this movie. I gave her the opportunity at the big time. Telling her all the time she should choose another movie to bank role but alas, Ha,ha, her stubbornness would not let me dictate her choice. Then she did what I wanted her to do in the first place and during all this time she thought it was her idea. This part is my favorite. Now she will have no choice but to go to her father for some money.

Money I will use to make her a lot of money. Money she will take to her father. Then my time will come, when so fast I take everything away from the both of them. I'll stand there with my face so innocent and sweet, when I leave the company and I break our engagement."

(Voice talking to Jim that we cannot hear, confirms everything Jim needs to hear.)

"Last thing is my new starlet, the one that will be in my next movie ready to go."

(Voice talking to Jim that we cannot hear.)

"Good , good. Send her some flowers, with a note telling her to be ready in a week for us to get together and have some fun. I love my life, hang on a second. Damn here comes Jill just like a puppy wanting encouragement from me for her big scenes today. Guess I'll give her a bone to chew on as well she looks pretty hot, might as well enjoy myself. I'll make her look so sexy after we get it on, Ha.

33

She will glow for the camera, giving ammunition to you for her demise. Remember the pictures must only have her face not mine. Make sure they're time stamped so the whole world will know that right before she performed these scenes, she got laid. And real good at that if I say so myself. Give me ten minutes and I'll have her clothes off for you to get the pictures you need."

"Come on in Jill." "Good morning Jim, we got a big day today. How do I look?"

"You look good Jill." "Just good!?"

"Yeah Jill but if you want to look great close the door and take off your clothes."

"I don't know Jim, you might mess up my makeup."

"Don't worry Jill you are a star, I know the deal. I'll touch you just enough to get you turned on and ready for the day, our little secret that only we know. What do you say Jill? Do you want to look and feel just good? Or do you want me to make you feel and look great? It's all up to you Jill. You're the star, I just want to do my part to make you look even more starlet."

"Jim you are so good to me. I love you Jim. I really do even when I don't show it, you are still so deep in my heart. Jim my dear, I don't want you to think of it as helping me when you make love to me. I want you to think that you are making love to me for us. For Jim, when I am on top you will be right there behind me basking in my light. Oh Jim I am so excited this is just the beginning, our next movie will be even bigger than this one."

"You got that completely right Jill. You Jill the grand star, me the hard working director. Together you and I will fly high in the sky. Jill my love, we will own Hollywood. Everybody will love you because you are so beautiful and to everybody's eyes you will be pure, which of course the both of us know better than that."

"Jim you are so bad, close the curtain, here I come baby, you better be ready to love me."

Book Sixteen: Sexual Amnesia (Pages 35-57)

(Side One)
301. Sexual Amnesia (749.)
302. Inhale My Love (672.)
303. Where Is She Now (673.)
304. Shy Town (677.)
305. Sex Dance (678.)

(Side Two)
306. Love Bone (679.)
307. I'm A Little Small (Even Though I'm Pretty Tall) (674.)
308. 30 Minute Lady (684.)
309. Out The Window (Naked And Swinging) (704.)
310. Leave Her Man (705.)

(Side Three)
311. Fire Love (685.)
312. Fresh (724.)
313. Bump And Go (726.)
314. You Have A Lot Of Money (738.)
315. Give My Heart Away (746.)

(Side Four)
316. Let's Have A Party On The Floor (754.)
317. It's The Least I Can Do /
     How Have You Been Doing Baby (756.)
318. Call Me After (757.)
319. Cheater (758.)
320. Do You Like This (759.)

(Bonus Songs)
Bad Loving Lady (769.)
Un-Love (779.)

301. Sexual Amnesia

Hello – Did-We-Have – Sex-Together
Can't-Seem to Remember – I'm-Sure
One-More-Time – Might-Just-Make-Me
Remember – How-Much – I-Enjoyed-You

That's-It-Baby – 1-2-3 – Lose-All-Control
I'm so In-The-Need of Remembering a
Soft – Hot – Sexual – Experience

(Chorus)
Don't Tell Me Your Name
Just Give Me Your Body
I Have A Bad Case Of
Sexual Amnesia – Baby
Please Help Me To Remember
Even If It Takes – All-Day And All Night

Come-On – Sweet-Thing – Take-Me – All the Way
Shake-Your-Body – Don't-Hold-Back – Cure-My
Sexual-Amnesia – Don't-Give-Up-Baby

You're so Close – That's it Baby – Get-Hot
Lose-All-Control – I'm so In the Need
Of Remembering a Soft-Hot – Sexual-Experience

(Chorus)
Don't Tell Me Your Name
Just Give Me Your Body
I Have A Bad Case Of
Sexual Amnesia – Baby
Please Help Me To Remember
Even If It Takes – All-Day And All Night

Hello – Did-We-Have – Sex-Together
Can't-Seem to Remember – I'm-Sure
One-More-Time – Might-Just-Make-Me
Remember – How-Much – I-Enjoyed-You

That's-It-Baby – 1-2-3 – Lose-All-Control
I'm so In-The-Need of Remembering a
Soft – Hot – Sexual – Experience
(Repeat Chorus)

302. Inhale My Love

Baby – You're so Lonely
You're-Completely – Love-Starved
I-Can-Feel – Your-Tension
Baby-You-Need to Love-Out
Just-Let-Yourself – Go
Look at My-Body – Baby
I'm so Fine – I'm so Right
I'm-Built to Give – Out-Love
To-Ladies – That-Are – Starving-For-Love
Each and Every – Single-Night

(Chorus)
That's It Baby – Come And Get Me
Hold On Tight
Inhale My Love
I Got The Good Stuff
That Will Make You Feel
Like You Are Love-Stuffed
Inhale My Love Baby
I Will Make You So Love-High
From Inhaling – My-Thick-Hard-Love

You-Took a Hit – Off of My-Love
It-Made-You-Feel – So-Love-High
You-Gorged on My – Love-Bong
Never-Choking – Even-Once
I'm so Proud of You Baby
Looking so Sexy-Sweetheart – Laying-There
In a Love-Daze – Like-This is The-Way
Life-Should – Always-Be

(Chorus)
That's It Baby – Come And Get Me
Hold On Tight
Inhale My Love
I Got The Good Stuff
That Will Make You Feel
Like You Are Love-Stuffed
Inhale My Love Baby
I Will Make You So Love-High
From Inhaling – My-Thick-Hard-Love

303. Where Is She Now

I-Played-With-Love
For so Very-Long
Never-Really – Wanting-It to Stick
To-My-Heart – Like-Glue

When-I-Feel – The-Almost-Passion
Of-Love – Creeping-Into-My-Heart
I-Always-Take-Off – The-Morning-After
I-Told-Them – Goodbye-Twice
The-Night-Before – Oh-Yeah

(Chorus)
Where Is She Now
She Was So Nice
I Took Off My Clothes
She Took Off Hers
Like She Wanted Me
As Much As I Wanted Her
If-She Was Here Now – We'd Be Naked

She-Found – Her-Man in Me
I-Tried to Tell-Her
I'm-Not the Loving – Kind of Man
After-Making-Love – But-She
Wanted-No-Part in That
Telling-Me – I'm-Making a Mistake

Next-Day – I-Laughed – It-All-Away
Like-My-Love for Her – Was-Not-True
Years-Later – I'm so Very-Lonely
Her-Face-Is on My-Mind as Her-Heart
Belongs to Someone-Else – Oh-No

(Chorus)
Where Is She Now
She Was So Nice
I Took Off My Clothes
She Took Off Hers
Like She Wanted Me
As Much As I Wanted Her
If-She Was Here Now – We'd Be Naked

304. Shy Town

I'm-Glad – They're-Not-Me
Even-Though – I'm so Lonely
They-Stay-Away – From-Me
Like-I – Have a Disease

At-First – I-Tried to Score
All-The-Ladies – Just-Looked at Me
Like-I-Was – From-Yesterday
A-Yesterday – That is Best-Forgotten
Oh-What-This-Town – Has-Become

(Chorus)
I Live In A Shy Town
Where No One Has Sex
One By One They Arrived
Leaving Me The Only One Around
That Is Not Shy And In The Need Of
Having Lots And Lots Of Sex

In-This-Shy-Town – I'm-The-Only-One
That-Has A-Pool – A-Grill
Green-Grass – Pretty-Flowers
To-Look-At and Enjoy-In-The-Sun

I-Kissed – One of Them-Once
She-Tasted – Metallic
No-Passion in Her-Heart
No-Love – No-Lust in Her-Eyes
Oh-What-This-Town – Has-Become

(Chorus)
I Live In A Shy Town
Where No One Has Sex
One By One They Arrived
Leaving Me The Only One Around
That Is Not Shy And In The Need Of
Having Lots And Lots Of Sex

Help-Me – Save-Me – I'm in The-Need of Sex
Help-Me – Save-Me – Is-There-Anyone at Home
Help-Me – Save-Me – Where-Are-The-Horny-People

305. Sex Dance

You're-Good – I'm-Bad
You're-Pretty – I'm-Not
You-Want to Be-Loved
I-Want-You – For an Hour

Baby – Glory is In-My-Pants
It's-Great to Want-It
All-You – Gotta-Do-Is
Join-Me – In a Sweet – Sex-Dance

(Chorus)
Sex Dance With Me Baby
I'll Spin You Around And Around
So Many Times – You'll Melt
In My Arms – As You
Sex Dance With Me Baby

1-2-3 Baby – Here-We-Go
That's it Baby – Let's-Start-Slow
With a Sexy-Slow – Sex-Dance
Let-Me-Lead – Give-Yourself to Me

With-Me in Control – Baby
All-You-Have to Do is Pant
Keep-Your-Part of Our
Sex-Dace – Going-On and On
'Til-I-Feel – The-Time is Right
To-Change – Sex-Dancing-Partners

(Chorus)
Sex Dance With Me Baby
I'll Spin You Around And Around
So Many Times – You'll Melt
In My Arms – As You
Sex Dance With Me Baby

You're-Good – I'm-Bad – You're-Pretty – I'm-Not
You-Want to Be-Loved – I-Want-You – For an Hour
Baby – Glory-Is – In-My-Pants – It's-Great
To-Want-It – 'Cause-All-You – Gotta-Do-Is
Join-Me – In a Sweet – Sex-Dance
(Repeat Chorus)
40

306. Love Bone
(If You Don't Love My Love-Bone – Then You Don't Love Being Boned)

Sex-On-My-Mind
Love-Bone in My-Pants
I'm-Doing-Fine – Tonight
Let's-Dance-Baby – Let's-Dance
Let-Me – Turn-You-On

Yeah-Baby – It's-All-Real
When-We-Get – All-Alone
I'll-Show-You – My-Love-Bone
Love-It-Baby – I'll-Even-Let-You-Feel-It
I'm-That-Kinda – Amazing

(Chorus)
Thank Your Body Baby
For Your Great Time
You're So Welcome
I Know You Love
My Love Bone
But Baby – Oh Baby
My Love Bone
Will Never Be Satisfied
With Only One Love Slice

I'm a Hard-Bad-Man – That-Can-Go
I'll-Make-You so Happy
Then-I'll-Make-You so Sad
When-I-Put – My-Love-Bone
Back-In-My-Pants
Welcome to The-Way-It-Is
Where-I-Come – Then-I-Go

(Chorus)
Thank Your Body – Baby
For Your Great Time
You're So Welcome
I Know You Love
My Love Bone
But Baby – Oh Baby
My Love Bone
Will Never Be Satisfied
With Only One Love Slice
41

307. I'm A Little Small (Even Though I'm Pretty Tall)

Sweet-Lady – Don't-Worry
About-What I-Lack – Where-It
Matters-The-Most – So-Sad-Indeed
But-I'm-Very – Wealthy-Clean

I-Have a Large-Account
That-Will – Turn-You-On
Making-You – Want to Stay
Even-When – You-Don't-Get
Turned-On – Where-You
Want-It-The-Most

(Chorus)
I'm A Little Small
Even Though I'm Pretty Tall
This Might Seem Unfair To Me
But I'm Richer Than You
Which Makes Me Better Than You
Even With Your Poor Large-Sizes
That You Enjoy – Like Rutting Pigs

Let-Me-Tell-You – Mister-Poor
Don't-You – Get-Any-Ideas
'Cause-I – Never-Share
Look and Want – Then-Look-Away
Because-I'm – Aware of You

Even if My-Lady – Says-Yes
You-Better – Say-No-Thanks
You-Touch – I'll-Make-You-Pay
Homage to My – Large-Bank-Account

(Chorus)
I'm A Little Small
Even Though I'm Pretty Tall
This Might Seem Unfair To Me
But I'm Richer Than You
Which Makes Me Better Than You
Even With Your Poor Large-Sizes
That You Enjoy – Like Rutting Pigs

42

308. 30 Minute Lady

She-Don't-Ask – How-I'm-Doing
She-Doesn't-Even-Care
As-Long-As-I'm – Long-And-Tall
She's a Happy – 30-Minute-Lady

With-Her-Hurry-Up – Give-It to Me
I-Have to Be-Going – Right-After
That-She-Says to Me – Over and Over
Like a Fine-Ass – Stuck-Record

(Chorus)
Love Is Not A Option
She's The 30 Minute Lady
With Another Life To Live
I'm Just The Right Before
She Has The Home To Go To
Thinking About Her 30-Minutes
Her-Time That Makes Life
Worth-Living – Every Single Day

This-Day-I-Don't – Feel-The-Same
I-Wanna-See – What-Happens-When
My-30-Minute-Lady – Becomes-My
Two to Three-Hour – Until-I'm
Done-With-Her – This-Time-Lady

1 Hour-Into-Our-Loving – She's-Saying-Hurry-Please
2 Hours-Later – She's-Saying – You're-Getting-Me in Trouble
3 Hours-Later – She-Tells-Me – I-Ruined-Her-Life
30 Minutes-Later – She is No-Longer – My-30-Minute-Lady
After-I-Told-Her – Thank-You – Goodbye and So-Long

(Chorus)
Love Is Not A Option
She's The 30 Minute Lady
With Another Life To Live
I'm Just The Right Before
She Has The Home To Go To
Thinking About Her 30-Minutes
Her-Time That Makes Life
Worth-Living – Every Single Day

309. Out The Window (Naked And Swinging)

I-Like-The-Ladies – The-Ladies-Like-Me
I-Got-What it Takes – For a Good-Time
Love-'Em – Leave- 'Em – That's-My-Way
I-Like to Party – With-My-Clothes-Off

It's-Not-My-Fault – If-They-Don't-Tell
'Cause-I-Don't-Ask – I'm-Free
Ladies-Look at Me – And-Smile
Knowing-I'm-Just-What – They-Need so Bad

(Chorus)
Grab My Pants
Pick Up My Shirt
Leave Behind My-Shorts
Here I Am Once Again – Going Out
The Window – Naked And Swinging

Ladies-Ask – Sometimes-I-Say-Yes
Looks-Are – The-Most-Important to Me
I'm-Not-Looking to Get-Married
Just-Enjoy – What-They-Have to Offer

I'm-Not-Looking to Stay – She's-Yours
I'm-The-Thing – She-Needs
To-Keep-Her-Around and Begging
Being-Satisfied – With-Some-Needed-Lust
So-She-Don't – Go-Looking-For-Love

(Chorus)
Grab My Pants
Pick Up My Shirt
Leave Behind My-Shorts
Here I Am Once Again – Going
Out The Window – Naked And Swinging

Now-She-Sees-Me – Now-You-Don't
I'm-Done – Putting-On-My-Clothes
Does-She-Still – Love-You
I-Don't-Know – and – I-Don't-Care
'Cause -Mister-Lacking – That's-Your
Problem-Man – Not-Mine
(Repeat Chorus)
44

310. Leave Her Man

I-Just-Got-Laid – Feeling so Fine
I-See-You – Man-You're so Blue
Looking-Way-Down – In-The-Dumps
All-Because – Your-Lady is Cheating

I-Could be Nice – But-I-Won't
You-Kinda-Deserve-This – She's-Way
Out of Your-League to Please-Her
She-Just-Loves – Your-Money
So-Man – I'm-Going to Tell-You-This

(Chorus)
Leave Her Man
She Cheats On You – All The Time
Anytime – Anywhere – I Should Know
'Cause She Cheated With Me – More Than Once
Who Knows – Maybe Even Again Tomorrow

Man-That is Blue – You're-Turning-Red
Anger-For-Me – In-Your-Heart
You-Boast to Destroy-My-World
While-Yours is Already-Destroyed

I-Understand – I-Get-It
From-The-Other-Side – But-Still
I-Feel-Your-Pain – Tell-You-What-Man
I-Got-It – Just-What-You-Need
To-Understand – Your-Problem

Find a Lady – That-Will-Love-You
She'll-Be-Not – So-Pretty-Looking
But-That's-Okay – Because
She'll-Be-The-One – Just-For-You
That-Nobody-Else – Wants

(Chorus)
Leave Her Man
She Cheats On You – All The Time
Anytime – Anywhere – I Should Know
'Cause She Cheated With Me – More Than Once
Who Knows – Maybe Even Again Tomorrow

45

311. Fire Love

We-Got to Talk Baby
Friend of Mine – Was-Talking
To a Friend of Yours
She-Told-The-Tale of How-I'm-Not
Keeping-Your – Fire-Lit

I'm-Slowly – Cooling-You-Down
Causing-You to Frown
I-Didn't-Know – This-Baby
'Cause-I'm – On-Cloud-Nine
While-You're – Drifting-Calmly

(Chorus)
Your Search For Fire Love
Takes You Away From My Love
I Hope You Find A Love
That Burns Your Soul
Your Very Own Fire Love
That Lights Your Fire

Such a Shame – It's-Come to This
I-Want-You to Be-Happy
So-Baby-Pack – Your-Bags
Leave-Me-Today – But-Baby
On-Your-Way – Out-The-Door
I've-Have to Tell-You-This

Your-Search – For-Fire-Love
Will-Not-Lead-You-Back – To-My-Door
Blame-Your-Passion – Not-Mine
For-You-Had-True-Passion – Loving-You
That-You-Did-Not – Really-Love

(Chorus)
Your Search For Fire Love
Takes You Away From My Love
I Hope You Find A Love
That Burns Your Soul
Your Very Own Fire Love
That Lights Your Fire

312. Fresh

You-Like – My-Face
I-Like – Your-Ass
Let's-See – How-We-Look
With-Our-Clothes – On-The-Floor

That-Was-Great – Lust-You-Later
Can't-Stay – Any-Longer
My-Time – With-You is Up
I-Already-Need – More-Fresh

(Chorus)
Searching – I'm Searching
Looking For A Great Time
I Need Constantly Fresh
To Ease My Mind – To Slate My Soul
Fresh Let's Roll On Along
So I Can Find More Fresh
To Make My Body – Quiver And Shake
So Baby Give Me All Your Fresh
'Til You Have No More Fresh To Give Me

Pull-Up – Your-Shirt
Pull-Down – Your-Skirt
Do-You-Have – What-I-Need
To-Make-Me – Smile and Pant

More-Than-Okay – Not to Tell-Me
Your-Name – Your-Address
'Cause-I-Really – Don't-Care
Unless-You – Have a Fresh-Friend
That-Won't-Mind – Knowing-Me-For-Awhile

(Chorus)
Searching – I'm Searching
Looking For A Great Time
I Need Constantly Fresh
To Ease My Mind – To Slate My Soul
Fresh Let's Roll On Along
So I Can Find More Fresh
To Make My Body – Quiver And Shake
So Baby Give Me All Your Fresh
'Til You Have No More Fresh To Give Me
47

313. Bump And Go

I-Wish – She-Told-Me
When-I-First – Met-Her
That-She – Was a Slut
It-Would-Have – Saved-Me
A-Whole-Lot of Time

I-Would-Have – Showed-Up
With-My-Pants-Off
Instead of Taking-Her to Dinner
I-Would-Have – Fed-Her
My-Delicious – Tube-Snake

(Chorus)
Sometimes Life's A Bitch
Sometimes You Date A Slut
You Just Never Know
What Life Will Throw At You
So Be Ready To Bump And Go
Just In Case She Bumps A Lot

I-Guess – I -Should be Happy
At-Least – She-Didn't-Give-Me
The-Clap to Walk-Around-With
Like an Enemy – Inside-Me

She-Called-Me – The-Other-Day
Said-She-Was-Sorry – Said-She-Was-Lonely
I-Said – I'd-Give-Her – One-Night
'Cause – I'll-Bump a Slut
I-Just-Won't – Date-One

(Chorus)
Sometimes Life's A Bitch
Sometimes You Date A Slut
You Just Never Know
What Life Will Throw At You
So Be Ready To – Bump And Go
Just In Case – She Bumps A Lot

End of Story – So-Bump-Off
See-You – Next-Week-Baby

48

314. You Have A Lot Of Money

You-Come-Home – Tired-From-Cheating
Look-Me in My – Eyes and Say
I-Love-You-Baby
What's-For-Dinner – I'm-Starving
First-I-Need a Shower – Then-I'll-Eat
Here's-Some-Flowers – Just-For-You

(Chorus)
You Have A Lot Of Money
I Enjoy Spending It
You Have A Lot Of Money
You Are A Lousy Lover
You Have A Lot Of Money
I'm Going To Dump Your Ass
– – – – – – –
You Have A Lot Of Money
I'm Going Out To Get Laid
You Have A Lot Of Money
I Want All Of It
You Cheating Bastard

You-Come-Home – Tired-From-Cheating
Smelling-Like – Another-Lover
I-Give-You – An-Empty-Plate
Empty as You – Made-My-Heart
I-Leave-You – With-Your-Mouth-Wide-Open
With-All-Your-Money – In-Bag #2
I-Hope-You're-Happy – You-Lousy-Lover

(Chorus)
You Have A Lot Of Money
I Enjoy Spending It
You Have A Lot Of Money
You Are A Lousy Lover
You Have A Lot Of Money
I'm Going To Dump Your Ass
– – – – – – –
You Have A Lot Of Money
I'm Going Out To Get Laid
You Have A Lot Of Money
I Want All Of It
You Cheating Bastard

315. Give My Heart Away

Why-Am-I-Here – On-My-Mind
As-I-Drink – This-Drink
Puffing-On a Cigarette
Laughing-Inside at The-Ladies
That-Want-Me to Take-Them-Home

No-Way – That-Won't-Do – Not-Tonight
My-Heart is Broken to Pieces
Since-My-Lady-Left-Me – High-And-Dry
When-Her-New-Lover – Made-Her-Happier in Bed

(Chorus)
I Did Nothing But – Give My Heart Away
When It Was All About My Package
She Loved It – But She's A Nympho
I Heard She Screws Around On The Guy
She Screwed Around On Me With
She's Such A Get Around Nympho Lady
Spreading Her Legs For Lots Of Pleasure
Let's Cheer For Her – (Go-Go – Go-Away – Nympho Lady)

I-Figure – Payback-Should-Be a Bitch
Just-Like – She-Turned-Out to Be
So-I-Screwed – Her-Friends
Then-I-Screwed – Her-Sisters
Her-Mom – Was-Still-Hot
So-I-Gave-Her – What-She-Wanted
Then-I-Realized – That-I'm a Nympho-To

So-I-Called – My-Cheating-Ex
Told-Her To Come-Over and Screw-Me
Because – I-Don't-Give a Damn – Any-More

(Chorus)
I Did Nothing But – Give My Heart Away
When It Was All About My Package
She Loved It – But She's A Nympho
I Heard She Screws Around On The Guy
She Screwed Around On Me With
She's Such A Get Around Nympho Lady
Spreading Her Legs For Lots Of Pleasure
Let's Cheer For Her – (Go-Go – Go-Away – Nympho Lady)

316. Let's Have A Party On The Floor

Alone and Drunk – Feeling-Way-Down
Where-Are-The-Ladies – That-Like to Rock
Where-Have-These – Ladies-All-Gone
Miss-Their – Sweet-Spots so Much

Older-Maybe – But-Still-Always – Ready to Go
On-The-Floor – Having-Wild-Sex
I'll-Be-Willing – To-Keep-Doing-This
'Til-The-Day – I-Sex-Myself to Death

(Chorus)
Come On Hot Ladies – That Like Sex
Let's Have A Party On The Floor
I Am a Real – Go Get Her
Then Her – Then Her
Why Hesitate One Bit Ladies
Let's Have A Party On The Floor
Then It Will Be – Your Turn To Be Gotten

Saturday-Night – Phone-Rings
About-Damn-Time – I'm-Horny-Here
Ladies – Yes-Ladies – I-Can-Come-Over
How-Many-Are-You – Never-Mind – Doesn't-Matter

What is That-Ladies – You-Want-Me to Wear – What
Sorry-Ladies – Don't-Own-One of Those – But
Ladies o' Ladies – I-Have a Birth-Day-Suit
That-Will-Drive-You – Sexy-Wild
So-What-You-Say-Ladies – Yes or Yes

(Chorus)
Come On Hot Ladies – That Like Sex
Let's Have A Party On The Floor
I Am a Real – Go Get Her
Then Her – Then Her
Why Hesitate One Bit Ladies
Let's Have A Party On The Floor
Then It Will Be – Your Turn To Be Gotten

51

317. It's The Least I Can Do / How Have You Been Doing Baby

It's The Least I Can Do

We're-Alone at Last
From-My-Heart – I-Lust-You
You're-Shaking-Baby
This-Is a Big – Deal to You
I-Understand – This so Much
This is Not – My-First-Time
Even-Though – It's-Yours

(Chorus)
Take My Hand
Take Off Your Clothes
I Know Just What To Do
You Will Enjoy It – More Than Me
But That's Okay Baby
It's The Least I Can Do
To Get You Started – On Your Way Exploring
The World Of Hot Free Sex

(Repeat Both)

How Have You Been Doing Baby

Years-Fly-By – While-Getting-Laid
I-Can't – Complain at All
Even-When-It's – I've-Had-Better-Before
Out-There is The-Best – Just-Like-I-Am
I-Will-Find-Her – And-I-Will-Lay-Her
Wait a Minute – She-Looks – Very-Sexy-Familiar

(Chorus)
How Have You Been Doing Baby
Remember Me – Your First Lay
You Still Look – Very-Sex-Able Baby
Why Don't We Go – Somewhere And Screw
I Like To Check Out – How Far Your
Sex-Exploring – Has Taken You – Around This World

(Repeat Both)

52

318. Call Me After

I'll-Say – Yes to You
If-You – Don't Beg-Me
All-Over – My-New-Dress
Mister-Want-Me so Very-Much

You-Say-It-To-Me – Just-Like-The-Rest
Like-I-Haven't – Heard it All-Before
Know-This – Mister-Want-Me
I-Get-Bored – Very-Easy – Very-Fast – So-Just
Give-It to Me – Without-All-The-Talking

(Chorus)
Yeah – Yeah – Yeah
I Know You Like My Body
Every Mister Want Me Does
Just Give Me What I Need
Don't Fall In Love With Me
Or Call Me After

I-Don't-Need-You – You-Need-Me
You-Get-Three-Minutes – Now-Go

Not-The-Best – Of a Start so Far
I'm-Not – Getting-Turned-On
Your-Foreplay is Lacking-Style
Bad-Connection – You're-Out of Here

You-Yes-You – It's-Your-Turn to Try
Don't-Give-Me – That-Look – Like-I'm a Bitch
I-Want – What-I-Want – Don't-Care
If-You-Can't-Handle a Woman – That-Only
Wants-One-Thing – From a Man

(Chorus)
Yeah – Yeah – Yeah
I Know You Like My Body
Every Mister Want Me Does
Just Give Me What I Need
Don't Fall In Love With Me
Or Call Me After

319. Cheater

You-Look-Tired – Your-Hair is Messed-Up
Where-Have-You-Been
Out-With-The-Girls – You're-Tipsy
You're-Walking – Kinda-Funny

Leave-You-Alone – Not-Your-Fault
It-Was-The-Girls and Their-Boys
You-Didn't-Want to Stand-Out-All-Alone
Well-Baby – I-Was-Here
Willing and Wanting to Have a Good-Time

(Chorus)
You Are A Cheater
You Cheat All The Time
Don't Know Why I Even Bother
You Are A Cheater
Always Wanting To Take Off Your Clothes
Get Your Cheating Ass – Out Of Here

Don't-Want to Hear – Your-Excuses
Dirty-Dirty – Cheater
Now-That – I-Think-About-It
Looking at You – Like-This
You-Look – All-Used-Up
Not-Like-You – Did-Before

Well-All-I-Have to Say – Is-Baby
All-Your-Cheating – Has-Led-You
One-Step – Closer-To a Woman
That-Ain't-Worth-My-Time – See-You-Baby

(Chorus)
You Are A Cheater
You Cheat All The Time
Don't Know Why I Even Bother
You Are A Cheater
Always Wanting To Take Off Your Clothes
Get Your Cheating Ass – Out Of Here

320. Do You Like This

I-Just-Don't-Know – Any-More
Is it Me – I-Try – My-Best
But-You-Never – Seem to Want
To-Stick-Around – After-Baby
Like-You – Have-Somewhere to Go

I'm-Half-Proud but I-Feel-Jaded
Like-Every-Time – We-Get it On
You're-Just-There – For the Motions
Like-You-Owe-Me – Something
Well-Baby – How-About-This

(Chorus)
Do You Like This
Do You Like That
Is It Me – Is It Him
Which One Baby
Never Mind – Forget That
Baby Go Ahead – Hit The Road
'Cause Baby – I Don't Want You Any More

I-Feel-Better – You-Look-Like-Crap
He-Dropped-You – Just-Like-That
That-Puts a Smile – On-My-Face
Can't-Help it Baby – Can't-Feel-For-You

I-Was-Here – Ready-For-You to Stay
But-You-Wanted to Keep on Leaving
What-Do-You-Want – Baby
It's-Not-Like – I'll-Take-You-Back

(Chorus)
Do You Like This
Do You Like That
Is It Me – Is It Him
Which One Baby
Never Mind – Forget That
Baby Go Ahead – Hit The Road
'Cause Baby – I Don't Want You Any More

(Bonus Song)

Bad Loving Lady (769.)

Wish-I-Was a Magic-Man
Knowing-How to Use – My-Crystal-Balls
Then-Out of Nowhere – I-Would-Know
When-She-Would be Coming – After-My-Heart

She-Makes-Me – Feel so Great
She-Makes-Me – Feel so Loved
Then-Bam – I-Get-The-Love
Ripped-Right – Out of My-Heart

(Chorus)
She's Such A Bad-Bad
Bad Loving Lady
Always Looking For A Heart To Break
Just To Satisfy Her Dark Love
She's Such A Bad-Bad
Bad Loving Lady
Always Looking For A Heart To Eat-Raw
Out Of A Man's – In Love With Her Chest

I-Beg – She-Laughs – Wanting-More and More
I-Walk-Away – From-Her-Dark-Love
She-Shakes-Her – Fine-Ass-So-Fine
Making-Me-Say to Myself – Dark-Love-It

She-Makes-Me – Feel so Great
She-Makes-Me – Feel so Loved
Then-Bam – I-Get-The-Love
Ripped-Right – Out of My-Heart

(Chorus)
She's Such A Bad-Bad
Bad Loving Lady
Always Looking For A Heart To Break
Just To Satisfy Her Dark Love
She's Such A Bad-Bad
Bad Loving Lady
Always Looking For A Heart To Eat-Raw
Out Of A Man's – In Love With Her Chest

56

Un-Love (779.)

I-Like it Hot – I-Like it Alive
Love-Pounding in My-Heart
Is-It-For-Real – Am-I a Fool
For-Not-Believing-In – Un-Love
Where-Does it Come-From
How-Long – Has it Been-Here
Is-There-Anyway – To-Stop-It
From-Spreading-Itself – Out of Control
Has-This-World – Not-Bled-Enough

(Chorus)
Un-Love – Un-Love
Puts Hate In Your Heart
Un-Love – Un-Love
Is Love's Worst Enemy
Un-Love – Un-Love
Will Freeze Your Soul
Un-Love – Un-Love
Love It Too Good – Then Die Real Bad

Out of The-Corner of My-Eyes
I-See-It –There-It-Is – Un-Love
Freezing-Up – Someone's-Love
Licking-Its-Lips – Ready to Start
Devouring-Love – Like-It's-Meaty-Candy

Breath-Frozen – Watching in Fright
Un-Love is Vile and Love-Death-Hungry
Fire-In-My-Soul – Fuels-Out-Love – I'm-Ready
Come-On-Un-Love – Eat-My-Love and Choke-On-It

(Chorus)
Un-Love – Un-Love
Puts Hate In Your Heart
Un-Love – Un-Love
Is Love's Worst Enemy
Un-Love – Un-Love
Will Freeze Your Soul
Un-Love – Un-Love
Love It Too Good – Then Die Real Bad

Story Three: Sid, Candy and April
(Fred and May)

"Have you heard from him Candy?"

"No April, and I am glad that he hasn't called. He was fine for moments but just like every man I meet there is something missing in him that lets me know that he was just another one, that in the end, would not be there for me. So I let him buy me enough stuff. I let him get off just enough then I told him we were through. Kinda funny when I think now, what the look on his face looked like.

Was he sad and mad?

Maybe a little, mostly he was like what? I gave him his fifteen minutes after we got done making love. I left him laying on the bed, got cleaned up and dressed then basically told him that was that, so long, goodbye, don't call me I'll call you maybe."

"You're so bad, Candy."

"No April, I want to be in love, I'm not living under a rock, sex is sex, I love it, got to have it." Just don't see the point in having sex with the same person over and over when there are so many men out there to replace the last one, just like that. Unless of course I feel like I'm falling in love. Then I taper it down making him almost ready to start begging me for sex then like the greatest girlfriend in the world, I let him have me. Makes his slow man mind think about what a great wife I would be for him. It's almost too easy isn't it April?"

"For you Candy, men drool over you, lucky bitch. I love you but it's not fair, I give my heart away, they say they want it. We have lots and lots of sex then they're gone. Sometimes I don't even get a phone call. One time I would like to be the one that drops them just like that, Candy."

"Well April, tonight is your lucky night." "I do not feel lucky Candy." "That is about to change April."

" What are you going to do Candy? Wave your hands in the air and make the Man of my dreams appear right out of thin air?"

"Better than that April, I'm going to start you on your way to being your own woman, a woman that controls her life including her love life."

"Just like that, Candy, what am I going to say out loud? I got it. See me world, I am woman hear me moan. What then? Do I then cry and bitch, blaming the world instead of myself? Been there done that."

"April you can do that I guess or you can stop your yapping and listen to the master of using men."

"Well grace me with you wise words Candy. Change me into the woman of my dreams, better yet change me into man's worst nightmare in a pair of tight pants."

"April you lucky Bitch, here is step one. April, You're still with that boring man of yours, that I have never met right?"

"Yes and he's not that boring, he's funny sometimes he..."

"Shut up April, you're making my panties bunch up from hearing those pathetic words coming out of your mouth."

"Well Candy if you don't like those words, I still have two more words for you, I would love to say to you right now, bitch."

"Okay then, bitch, it goes like this. Call that boring man of yours up and tell him to come over here."

"Why would I want to do that Candy?"

"April if you want this to work, no questions, just do as I say and after that you will be ready for step two."

"Okay Candy, I guess my T & A is in your hands."

"Call him April, tell him to come over. That's it, make him wonder what's going on, let his mind get him all excited. April this is going to be so great, when he gets here we're going to open the door all sexy looking, then we are going to... "

(Sid)

Sid's been getting it real good from April, he likes her a lot but he has been wondering if she is the girl for him. Lately and secretly Sid has been putting himself out there trying to find another lover or two. Sid has had some luck, couple of them were almost tens in bed, but what needy ladies they were. Sid knows with ladies like this he would have no alone time to have a beer with his friends. So like the smart man Sid is he slept with them once or five times, letting every one of them think his name is Fred instead. Fred, I mean Sid is just about to take off, there is one lady named May that he has enjoyed three times and a fourth time, right now sounds very good to Sid. Sid picks up his phone to give her a call to see if she is ready to meet him in their special place, when his phone rings in his hand.

(One Hour Later) Sid is knocking on the door belonging to his lover April's friend. Sid thinks, this is a nice part of town, lady has money, maybe I'll come back over all alone and introduce myself again as Fred. Hope She's hot and does it all, yeah right lady's probably a nice lady if you know what I mean. A nice to meet you, never will I want to see you naked type of lady, no thank you, please. Three knocks, no answer. Wonder what's up with that? What is behind this door that will consume my night, tonight? (Foot steps) Damn I'm horny.

"Hello, big man Sid, come in if you can!" "What the Sex April? What are you wearing? Damn, girl you look so sexy, sexy, fine, let me taste you." "Hold on, big man Sid, this night is all under my control, I tell you when and if you even can taste me you hear me, Man Dog of lust." "April, I think you have flipped your lid, I'm all in to playing while having sex. Man Dog? Yeah right, crazy lady. Think you can get me to bark while you play with my bone? Nice try. You're fine, how does your friend look? Will she be joining us?"

"April, April, what a surprise you are. Got so many questions, let me inside and give me my answers."

"Come in big man Sid, but wipe your feet first." "Yes Queen so Fine."

Sid walks in and sees May, his three times, standing there wearing a teddy, she has worn before for him. Candy's smile drops from her lips as she is staring at Fred who is actually Sid. The same Sid that she had a date with tonight before April came over unannounced making her not answer her phone.

In Sid's mind, I'm Busted.) (In Candy's mind, he's my friend's man, but she is about to dump him, maybe he might not be so pissed off and still want to have sex with me.)

April looks confused, "Candy you're not playing your role. What's going on? Sid? Am I the one being played with like a fool? How could you do this to me, the both of you, how could you?"

Sid looks at Candy – Candy looks at Sid, they both shrug their shoulders. Candy starts up her role tonight with a new dialog, that changes everyone's life like an accident that was made to happen.

Candy shakes her head, "You heard your woman Sid, tell her what's going on. Tell her I am your Lady, how you seduced me with your manhood. Damn you Sid, April is my friend and my favorite month. Damn you Sid! Damn your Manhood, that feels like it's been blessed by God himself. I am so weak, I am so sorry, April, I am so weak."

Sid looks at Candy and swallows, saying with his eyes, What! Sid shakes his head, grabs hold of his package then says out loud,

"Rock and Roll. That was great Candy now take April to the bedroom and tie her up with pairs of your panties. She'll be our new toy tonight, as we keep on exploring sex. And not just any sex I tell you. April my love, I am so glad that you are finally here to share this with us. Candy has been telling me how much she can't wait to get it on with you. This is her first time with another woman as well. And I am quoting Candy's exact words when I say this. If I am to ever do this it has to be in April, excuse me please, I mean with April."

Candy and April kiss, then they hold out their hands for Sid to take. Let your imagination roam free as to how this special loving moment between three people began and ended this night.

All I am willing to say is that the night ended with three people having great big smiles on their lips. This night has been repeated so much that the three of them are living together happily in blessed hot loving sin, that seems to get more loving each and every 3-Way day.

Book Seventeen: Party In Your Panties (Pages 62-85)

(Side One)
321. Party In Your Panties (830.)
322. Big Breasted Woman (Heaven Is In My Pants) (831.)
323. Teaser (821.)
324. What Is It Baby (851.)
325. Twisted While Horny (832.)

(Side Two)
326. Lies With Cries (186.)
327. Your Man (241.)
328. Desire (My Baby's Full Of Hell's Fire) (267.)
329. I Love You (Sorry Baby) (276.)
330. Feel Loved (290.)

(Side Three)
331. Show No Love (291.)
332. Left Behind For The Third Time (296.)
333. Starts To Get Good (316.)
334. I Was True When You Were Not (324.)
335. Sex Hungry Kinda Guy (325.)

(Side Four)
336. Lady Love Came Up To Me (326.)
337. She's A Total Destruction (334.)
338. Let Love Come Flowing Into My Heart (356.)
339. If You Say Yes Sexy Lady (374.)
340. Re-Grow My Love (395.)

(Bonus Songs)
Come On All You Sex Having People (532.)
A Sin A Day (Around The Corner Of Sex) (546.)
F.M.L. (Freeze My Love)
L.K.G. (Last Kiss Goodbye)

321. Party In Your Panties

We-Went-Out-Once – Sexed it Up-Twice
What a Night – I'll-Never-Forget
Time-Goes-By – I've-Forgotten-Your-Name
Out of The-Corner of My-Eye
I-See-Your-Body and Face
Standing-There – Ready to Be-Enjoyed

What-Else-Can-I-Do – But-Come-Up to You
Look-You – In-Your-Eyes – And-Say

(Chorus)
Baby I've Heard – Baby I've Heard
There's A Party In Your Panties – Tonight
Hope I'm The Only One – Invited
'Cause You Know – How I Hate To Share
What's In Your Panties – 'Til I'm Done

You-Slap-My-Face – I'm so Cruel
Out of The-Blue – I-Was-Rude
Giving-No-Thought – About-Your-Feelings
And-The-Man – Who-Shares-Your-Life

What-Can-I-Say-Baby – What-Can-I-Do
I'm a Man – That-Likes to Get-It-On
So-Let-Me-Repeat – Myself-To-You

(Chorus)
Baby I've Heard – Baby I've Heard
There's A Party In Your Panties – Tonight
Hope I'm The Only One – Invited
'Cause You Know – How I Hate To Share
What's In Your Panties – 'Til I'm Done

Baby-If-This-Makes – You-Feel-Better
Your-Man – Can-Have-You-Back – When-I'm
Done-With – Twice-More – Times-With-You

Fine-Once in My-Life – Before-You-Walk-Away
What-Else-Can-I-Do – But-Look at You
And-Say – One-More-Time

(Repeat Chorus)
63

322. Big Breasted Woman (Heaven Is In My Pants)

Big Breasted Woman
My Name Is Hard As A Rock
Big Breasted Woman
Come Sit On My Lap
Big Breasted Woman
Wave Your Big Breast In My Face
Big Breasted Woman
How's The Rest Of Your Body
Big Breasted Woman
I Like A Woman With Big Breast

Big Breasted Woman
Let's Walk The Sex Party
Big Breasted Woman
Let's Find Someone Special
For You To Share Me With
Big Breasted Woman
Look At Her Over There
Looking All Sexy And Ready
Big Breasted Woman
Take Off Your Shirt – Maybe She Will To

(CHANGES)

I'm So Special – I'm So Blessed
Heaven Is In My Pants
Pleasing Two Ladies At The Same Time
Heaven Is In My Pants
Think I'll Take Them Home With Me
Heaven Is In My Pants
Tomorrow Is Another Day For Having Sex
Heaven Is In My Pants

Wonder How Long I Can Keep This Going On
Heaven Is In My Pants
After A Month Will I Even Be Able To Walk
Heaven Is In My Pants
I'm So Special – I'm So Blessed
Heaven Is In My Pants
If I Die Happy And Smiling Tomorrow
Heaven Will Still Be In My Pants

323. Teaser

Let-Me – Tell-You-My-Story
I'm-Way-Up-High – She's-Way-Down-Low
I-Want to Score – She-Says – No-No-No
I'm-Out of Mind – From-Taking-Her-Slack
That-Never-Joins-Me – In-The-Sack

Come on Baby – Can't-You-Change
Be-The-Smiling – Be-The-Pleasing
Hot-Looking-Lady – That-I-Want to
Get-It-On-With – But-Instead

(Chorus)
Baby You're A Teaser
A Non-Pleasing Teaser
That Never Gets Turned On
Baby You're A Teaser
A Non-Pleasing Teaser
That Never Turns Me On
Such A Shame – What A Waste
You Would Look So Hot – Getting It On

Baby-I'm – To-Turned-On – Right-Now
To-Wait – Any-More-Baby
Stop-Being a Teaser
Please-Me – 'Til-You-Become a
Slack-Less in The-Sack
Lady of My – Hot-Loving-Dreams

Come on Baby – Can't-You-Change
Be-The-Smiling – Be-The-Pleasing
Hot-Looking-Lady – That-I-Want to
Get-It-On-With – But-Instead

(Chorus)
Baby You're A Teaser
A Non-Pleasing Teaser
That Never Gets Turned On
Baby You're A Teaser
A Non-Pleasing Teaser
That Never Turns Me On
Such A Shame – What A Waste
You Would Look So Hot – Getting It On

324. What Is It Baby

Hey-Baby – What-Is-It-Baby
That-Is-Turning-You-Off
Is-It-My-Face – Is-It-My-Love
Is-It-My-Heart – Is-It-My-Size
Oh-No – That's-Turning-You-Off

I-Don't-Know – That's so Sad
I-Don't-Know – Just-Want to Be-Turned-On
I-Don't-Know – Feel so Bad
I-Don't-Know – Just-Want-You to Be – Turned-On
I-Don't-Know and I-Have to Ask-You-This

(Chorus)
What Is It Baby – I Have To Do
What Is It Baby – That Will Turn You On
What Is It Baby – I Have To Do
What Is It Baby – That Will Turn You On
I Love You Baby – I Live To Be Turned On
Tell Me Baby – So I Can Turn You On
Tell Me Baby – Or I Gotta Get Going

Hey-Baby – What-Is-It-Baby
That-Is-Turning-You-Off
Is-It-My-Face – Is-It-My-Love
Is-It-My-Heart – Is-It-My-Size
Oh-No – That's-Turning-You-Off

I-Don't-Know – That's so Sad
I-Don't-Know – Just-Want to Be-Turned-On
I-Don't-Know – Feel so Bad
I-Don't-Know – Just-Want-You to Be – Turned-On
I-Don't-Know and I-Have to Ask-You-This

(Chorus)
What Is It Baby – I Have To Do
What Is It Baby – That Will Turn You On
What Is It Baby – I Have To Do
What Is It Baby – That Will Turn You On
I Love You Baby – I Live To Be Turned On
Tell Me Baby – So I Can Turn You On
Tell Me Baby – Or I Gotta Get Going

325. Twisted While Horny

Met-You – With-Roses-In-My-Hand
You-Smelled-Them and Smiled
Then-Threw-Them – On-The-Ground
Bit-Me on My-Cheek
While-Stomping – My-Roses to Mush
As-My-Blood – Dripped-Out of Your-Mouth

I-Taste-Great – I-Bleed-Good
I'm-Like a Fine-Wine – That-You
Want to Thirstily – Drink-Down

(Chorus)
Baby I Got To Say
You're One Mighty Fine Lay
But You're – Twisted While Horny
Baby I Got To Say
You're One Mighty Fine Lay
But You're – Twisted While Horny
I Just Don't Know What To Do
Okay One More Time – Then We're Through

I-Gave-You-Up – You-Said-No-Way
I-Told-You to Stay-Away
You-Laughed and Told-Me to Suffer
I-Said-Enough – Changed-My-Number
You-Came-Along and Set-My-Door on Fire

I-Asked-You – What-Will it Take
For-You to Set-Me-Free
You-Chomp-Down – On-Your-Teeth
Lick-Your-Lips – Pulled-Out-Your-Whip
I-Guess-I-Know – What-I'll-Be-Doing-Tonight

(Chorus)
Baby I Got To Say
You're One Mighty Fine Lay
But You're – Twisted While Horny
Baby I Got To Say
You're One Mighty Fine Lay
But You're – Twisted While Horny
I Just Don't Know What To Do
Okay One More Time – Then We're Through

326. Lies With Cries

I-Don't-Want – More-Lies
You-Did – What-You-Did
Just-Give-It – To-Me-Straight
I-Deserve – At-Least-That

Crying-That – You-Love-Me
Even-Though – You've-Been-Stepping-Out
Well so Sorry-For-You – Baby
Like a Fool – Your-Forgotten-Man
I-Did-Nothing – But-Stay-True

(Chorus)
I Gave You All That I Had
All The Love In My Heart
All You Give Back Is
Lies With Cries
Lies With Cries
That I Don't Want Anymore

Finally – You-Get it All-Out
You've-Been-Lonely – I'm-Away too Much
You-Start – Getting-That-Tone – Like-It's-My-Fault
Give-You a Few-Minutes – Enough to Let-You-Think
That-You – Got-Me – Right-Where – You-Want-Me
All-Nice and Wrapped-Around – Your-Finger

(Chorus)
I Gave You All That I Had
All The Love In My Heart
All You Give Back Is
Lies With Cries
Lies With Cries
That I Don't Want Anymore

Say to You-Baby – No-Way – We're-Through
I'm-Out of Here – So-Long to Your – Lies-With-Cries
Goodbye to-Your – Cheating-Ways-Baby
Here's to Never – Seeing-You-Again
I-Hope-Karma – Bites-You in Your-Heart
Don't-Call-Me – I'll-Call-You – Never

(Repeat Chorus)

327. Your Man

Sent-My-Last-Lady – Packing
She-Was-Becoming – The-Same
While-I'm-Looking-For a Change-Up
No-One-Is to Blame – It is What it Is
Now-I'm-Happy – To-Say-To-You

You-Want-Me – Been-Waiting-Years
To-Get-Your-Chance at Enjoying-Me
Great-Thing – Check-This-Out
Here-You-Go – I'm-Free
Do-Your-Best – Just-Go-For it Baby

(Chorus)
It's Your Lucky Day
I'm Free At Last
Just What You Always Wanted
For Me To Be Your Man
So Come On Over Pretty Lady
And I'll Give You Your Chance

Love-In-Your Eyes as You-Watch-Me
Drinking a Beer – After-Hours of Making-Love
Don't-Make-The-Same-Mistake – As-All-The-Others
I'm a Free-Man – Always-Will-Be
You-Will-Have to Learn to Share-Me

Cry and Hate – That-You-Love-Me
I-Understand it Happens – Every-Time
I-Find a New-Lover to Spend – Some-Time-With

You-Have to Find – Your-Peace – With-My-Love
No-One-Is to Blame – It is What it Is
Now-I'm-Happy – To-Say-To-You

(Chorus)
It's Your Lucky Day
I'm Free At Last
Just What You Always Wanted
For Me To Be Your Man
So Come On Over Pretty Lady
And I'll Give You Your Chance

328. Desire (My Baby's Full Of Hell's Fire)

We-Talk – I-Think-You-Want-Me
When-I-Try to Make – My-Move
You-Stop-Me-Cold – Making-Me-Remember
Our-Last-Time-Together to Keep-Me-Warm

Baby-You're so Hot and Cold
My-Emotions – Are-Overloading
As-You-Keep – Turning-Me-On
Shaking-With-Desire – Ready to Go
When-You-Decide it's Time
To-Turn-Down – Your-Flames

(Chorus)
Desire – I'm Full Of Desire
Damn Shame Because
My Baby's Full Of Hell's Fire
Desire – I'm Full Of Desire
Damn Shame Because
My Baby's Full Of Hell's Fire
All I Want To Do – Is Feel Her Heaven

Baby-You're so Hot and Cold
I-Don't-Mind – Freezing and Burning
Just so I-Can-Get – Close to You – But-I
Can't-Wait-Forever to Feel-Your-Heaven
'Cause-I'm a Man – That's-Full of Desire

Baby-Your-Hot is Very-Intense
But-Baby-Your-Cold – Matches it Exactly
Baby, oh Baby – You-Almost-Got-Me
Wrapped-Around – Your-Hell's-Fire
Such a Shame – I-Have to Walk-Away

(Chorus)
Desire – I'm Full Of Desire
Damn Shame Because
My Baby's Full Of Hell's Fire
Desire – I'm Full Of Desire
Damn Shame Because
My Baby's Full Of Hell's Fire
All I Want To Do – Is Feel Her Heaven

329. I Love You (Sorry Baby)

Sorry-Baby – For-Being – Such an Ass
Sorry-Baby – For-Being – Myself-Again
Sorry-Baby – I-Don't-Want to Fight
Sorry-Baby – It's-All-My-Fault

Sorry-Baby – Give-Me-Another-Chance
Sorry-Baby – I'll-Try-My-Best – Not to Mess-Up
Sorry-Baby – I-Want to Be-Happy-With-You
Sorry-Baby – Let's-Just-Hug and Kiss

(Chorus)
I Love You – I Love You Baby
I Want Things Back The Way They Were
Let's Forget What I Did
Let's Make Love Tonight
I Love You – I Love You Baby
I Want Things Back The Way They Were
Let's Forget What I Did
Let's Make Love Tonight

Sorry-Baby – For-Being – Such an Ass
Sorry-Baby – For-Being – Myself-Again
Sorry-Baby – I-Don't-Want to Fight
Sorry-Baby – It's-All-My-Fault

Sorry-Baby – Give-Me-Another-Chance
Sorry-Baby – I'll-Try-My-Best – Not to Mess-Up
Sorry-Baby – I-Want to Be-Happy-With-You
Sorry-Baby – Let's-Just-Hug and Kiss

(Chorus)
I Love You – I Love You Baby
I Want Things Back The Way They Were
Let's Forget What I Did
Let's Make Love Tonight
I Love You – I Love You Baby
I Want Things Back The Way They Were
Let's Forget What I Did
Let's Make Love Tonight

330. Feel Loved

Didn't-Have-Anyone – Lost-Without-Love
Afraid to Look-For-It – All-Alone-Watching
Love-Happening – All-Around to Everyone
Not-Allowing-Myself to Take a Taste of It

Love's-Been so Bitter to Me
I-Can't-Stand – It's-Taste-Anymore
Until-I-Found-You – Like a Dream
Allowing-Me – My-Chance to Say to You

(Chorus)
Cover Me Baby
I'm In The Need Of Love
The Feel Of Your Soft Body
Laying On Top Of My Hard Body
Makes Me Feel Loved

Not-Paying-Attention – In-Our-Own-World
We-Bump-Into-Each-Other – Making-Me-Spill
My-Hot-Coffee – On-Your-Pretty-Shoes
Did-My-Best – Not to Laugh
Watching-You-Do-Your – Hot-Feet-Dance

Mad as Hell – You-Look-Into-My-Eyes
Ready to Give-Me – What-I-Deserve
Love-Beams – From-My-Heart
Turns-Your-Frown – Upside-Down
When-You-See – The-Man of Your-Dreams
Allowing-Me – My-Chance to Say to You

(Chorus)
Cover Me Baby
I'm In The Need Of Love
The Feel Of Your Soft Body
Laying On Top Of My Hard Body
Makes Me Feel Loved

Cover Me Baby – I Need Love
Cover Me Baby – Make Me Feel Loved
Cover Me Baby – I Need Love
Cover Me Baby – Make Me Feel Loved

72

331. Show No Love

You-Say to Me – You'll-Change
That-Day – Never-Comes
It's-Always – The-Same-Way
You're-Filled – With-Frustrations
Making-My-Days – Full of Sorrow

I-Don't-Want – This to Go-On
'Cause – Life is Too-Short
Hanging-Around – With-Someone
That-Doesn't-Want to Have-Some-Fun

(Chorus)
The Pain Of The Day
Always Makes You Bring It
Right Down On Top Of Me
And I'm Tired Of Being The One
That You Show No Love To

I'm-The-One – That is Suppose
To-Be-Your – Only-One
Not-The-One – That-Takes-Your-Pain
You-Won't-Change – What-Can-I-Do
I-Have to Look – Out-For-Myself

Tears-In-My-Eyes of Years
That-Have – Passed-Us-By
I-Walk-Away – From-You
Hearing-You-Cry and Say
That-You – Will-Change-For-Me

Never – Understanding
That-You – Need to Change
For-Yourself – Not-Just-Me

(Chorus)
The Pain Of The Day
Always Makes You Bring It
Right Down On Top Of Me
And I'm Tired Of Being The One
That You Show No Love To

332. Left Behind For The Third Time

Never-Did-I-Think – I-Would-Feel-This-Bad
I'm a Three-Time-Loser
Wanted to Stay-Married – But-All-My-Others
Didn't-Want to Stay – With-My-Love
Leaving-Me – Now a Third-Time – Un-Charmed
World-Why – Is it Always-Me
That-Gets-Dumped – Like-Leftovers

(Chorus)
There Must Be Something Wrong
Maybe It's Me – I Don't Know
Guess It Has To Be Me
I'm The Only One That Got
Left Behind For The Third Time

I-Want to Love – Somebody-Special
Don't-Know-If-I-Can – Do-It a Fourth-Time
My-Spark-Has-Almost – Fizzled-Out
All-I-Want To-Do is Go-Inside-Myself and Hide
Like-The-Miserable – Unwanted-Lover
That is Not – Worth-Loving-Forever

(Chorus)
There Must Be Something Wrong
Maybe It's Me – I Don't Know
Guess It Has To Be Me
I'm The Only One That Got
Left Behind For The Third Time

Alone-Again – Staring at Empty-Walls
Only-The-Stuff in My-Mind to Comfort-Me
Sun-Shines – It-Still-Rains – Nobody-Ever-Calls
Laughing-Out-Loud – Drowning-Out – All-The-Silence
That's-Invaded – My-Heart – Like a Entity-That-Takes
My-Last-Bit of Love and Freezes it Solid

(Chorus)
There Must Be Something Wrong
Maybe It's Me – I Don't Know
Guess It Has To Be Me
For I'm The Only One That Got
Left Behind For The Third Time

333. Starts To Get Good

We-Agree – You-Love-Me
You're-Hot – Soft and Sweet
I'm-Ready – Hard and Spicy
Do-You – Want to Melt
No – What a Shame – Say-What
You're-Keeping-It – 'Til-You-Get Married

Well-Baby – Too-Bad-For-You
I'm-Not – The-Marrying-Type
I'm-The-If-You're – Great-Enough
I'll-Keep – Coming-Back for More
Type of Guy – You-Need to Love
Before-You Lose – Your-Chance at Perfection

(Chorus)
Even With The Way You Walk
You're All Talk And No Action
Giving Me Such Hot Kisses
Purring Like You Want Me
Then Moving Away Quickly
Right When It Starts To Get Good

You-Keep-Calling-Me – Wanting to Talk
When-Talking is The-Last-Thing – On-My-Mind
Cherry-Lady – You're so Fine
All-You-Have to Do is Say-Yes
I'll-Make-It – So-Very-Special
For-You and Your-First-Time

By-The-End of The-Night
You'll be So-Comfortable in Love
You-Will-Melt – With-Me-Anyway
Pleading in Between-Moans
For-Us to Never-Stop-Melting

(Chorus)
Even With The Way You Walk
You're All Talk And No Action
Giving Me Such Hot Kisses
Purring Like You Want Me
Then Moving Away Quickly
Right When It Starts To Get Good

334. I Was True When You Were Not

Everybody is Talking – About-The-Way-You
Dumped-Me – How-You-Enjoyed-Doing-It
Up-Close – Real-Mean and Nasty
Letting-Me-Have-It – Because-I-Cheated on You

How-Hot-You-Were – Walking-Away
Grabbing and Kissing a Stranger
Then-Leaving-With-Him – Calling-Me-Up
The-Next-Day – Telling-Me – What-You-Did
Like it Was – Some-Kind of Victory
Laughing – Then-Hanging-Up – Well

(Chorus)
I Gotta Tell You – Sorry My Ex-Love
I Was True When You Were Not
You Made A Big Mistake
By Listening To Your Friends
I Never Gave Myself To Someone Else
I Was True When You Were Not

Everybody is Talking – About-You – My-Ex-Love
How-You-Cried and Cried – All-Upset
Wanting-Me to Take-You-Back – Just-Like-That
Hoping – That-Your-Tears-Will-Change – My-Mind
Yeah-Right – Like-That's-Going to Happen – Well

(Chorus)
I Gotta Tell You – Sorry My Ex-Love
I Was True When You Were Not
You Made A Big Mistake
By Listening To Your Friends
I Never Gave Myself To Someone Else
I Was True When You Were Not

Don't-Worry-Ex-Love – I'm-Doing-Just-Fine
Here is The-Last-Thing – I-Have to Say
Lose-My-Number – We're-Through
Ain't-No-Way – I'll-Ever-Take-You-Back
I'm-Having a Great-Time – Dating-Your-Friends

(Repeat Chorus)

335. Sex Hungry Kinda Guy

I-Hear – How-Easy – It-Is to Fall
Deeply-Hard in Love
But-If-You – Want-It to Last
You-Have to Work-Hard – Everyday
So it Don't – Get-Old and Fade-Away
Dying-Like so Many – Others-Before-It

Always – Thinking to Myself
After-Hearing – This-Craziness
If-This is Love – You-Can-Have-It
I'll-Just-Have a Bunch of Sex-Instead
Let-Me-Explain – This to You-Baby

(Chorus)
I'm More Of The Flesh
Sex Hungry Kinda Guy
That Is Not Looking For Love
Only Hot Nights Of Hot Sexy-Sex
That I Can Boast About Later

I'm so Generous – I-Tell-You
Proving to Ladies – That a Night-Filled
With-Hot-Passionate – Sex-Making
Is so Much-Hotter – Without-Any-Love
Around to Screw-Up – The-Ecstasy of It-All

Loving – That-After Awhile – Love to Them
Is-Nothing-But-One – Big-Four-Letter-Word
That-They-Never – Want to Hear or Say-Again
In-Case-You-Forget – Baby-Sexy-Love
Let-Me-Explain – This to You-Baby
One-More – Sex-Having-Time

(Chorus)
I'm More Of The Flesh
Sex Hungry Kinda Guy
That Is Not Looking For Love
Only Hot Nights Of Hot Sexy-Sex
That I Can Boast About Later

336. Lady Love Came Up To Me

Putting-My-Ladies – On a Pedestal
Is-Very-Easy – I'm-The-Man
That is Great to Have a Great-Time-With
No-Tears – No-Promises – No-Lies
Just a Night to Receive – Full-Passion
That-Only-Comes-Around – Once-In a Lifetime

(Chorus #1)
Lady Love Came Up To Me – I Was Being Myself Again
Not Worrying About Anything – Just Being A Great Lover
Made Me Lose My Chance – At Finding True Love
I Did Not Care Enough – To Feel Anything But Lust

I'm-Out-Doing – My-Nightly-Thing
Having-My-Choice – Between-Three-Ladies
When-I-Hear – My-Name – Being-Called-Out
By a Sexy-Sweet-Soft-Voice – That-Sounds
So-Very-Familiar – But-I-Know in My-Mind
It's-Unfamiliar – So-I-Blocked-It-Out

(Chorus #2)
Lady Love Came Up To Me – I Was Not Ready For Love
Lady Love Came Up To Me – I Did Not Notice Her
Lady Love Came Up To Me – I Left Her Standing There All Alone
While I Walked Away – To Have A Night Full Of Hot Sex

This-Might-Very-Well – Be-All in My-Mind
Everything-Goes – Very-Quiet at Once
All-I-Can-Hear is The-Beating of My-Heart
Out of Nowhere – Like a Magical-Beacon
I-Hear-Her-Heartbeat – Calling-Out to Me
My-Mind-Clears – I-Believe-In-Love
I-Turn-Around – My-Lady-Love is Glowing-With-Love

(Chorus #3)
Lady Love Came Up To Me – I Was Ready For Love
Lady Love Came Up To Me – Looking Like A Slice Of Heaven
Lady Love Came Up To Me – Now I'm A One Woman Only Man
That Has The Best – Loving-Sharing – Every-Night

337. She's A Total Destruction

She's a Total-Destruction – I-Know-This – Believe-Me
Pain of Being-Hers – Is-Like-Paying a Tax
Just so I-Can-Be in Hell – Until-She-Finally-Decides to
Unwrap-Her-Heaven for Me – Letting-Me-Play for Awhile
Always-Taking it Away-From-Me – Before-I'm-Through-With-It

(Chorus)
She's A Total-Destruction
Making My Life And Heart
Feel Like They've Been Through
A Long-Hard – Bloody-Cold-War
That Only The Shake Of Her Ass
Can End My Pain And Torment

She's a Total-Destruction – I-Know-This – Believe-Me
She-Loves to Sink-Her – Fingernails in Real-Deep
Laughing and Moaning – As-She-Makes-Me-Bleed
She-Waits-Until – My-Wounds-Are-Almost-Healed
Then-She-Enjoys – Ripping-Them-Open-Again
Just so I-Can-Feel-The-Pain – Of-Loving-Her

(Chorus)
She's A Total-Destruction
Making My Life And Heart
Feel Like They've Been Through
A Long-Hard – Bloody-Cold-War
That Only The Shake Of Her Ass
Can End My Pain And Torment

She's a Total-Destruction – I-Know-This – Believe-Me
She-Loves to Make-Me-Beg – Having-Me-Kneel to Her
Altar of Sexual-Destructive-Love – She's a Hell-Cat
With a Sweet-Fine-Ass – She-Knows-For-Sure
That-She's in Total-Control – As-She-Makes-Me-Beg and Bleed

(Chorus)
She's A Total-Destruction
Making My Life And Heart
Feel Like They've Been Through
A Long-Hard – Bloody-Cold-War
That Only The Shake Of Her Ass
Can End My Pain And Torment

338. Let Love Come Flowing Into My Heart

I'm so Happy – I-Found-My – True-Love
My-Life is Finally – Going-My-Way
All-The-Bad – Has-Slipped-Away
Love is For-Me – I-Know it Now
About-Time – I'm-Finally-Doing
What-I've-Been – Needing to Do

(Chorus)
It Took A Long Time
I Had To Live Through Hell
Not Knowing What Love Could Do
'Til I Stopped Hating Myself And
Let Love Come Flowing Into My Heart

I-Love-Being in Love – I-Will-Keep-It
For-My-Heart – Needs-It – This-I-Know
When-My-Past-Life – Comes-Prancing-Back
I-Send it Back – Where it Belongs
Never-Allowing – Its-Darkness to
Make-Me-Remember – All-My-Scars

(Chorus)
It Took A Long Time
I Had To Live Through Hell
Not Knowing What Love Could Do
'Til I Stopped Hating Myself And
Let Love Come Flowing Into My Heart

I'm so Happy – I-Found-My – True-Love
My-Life is Finally – Going-My-Way
All-The-Bad – Has-Slipped-Away
Love is For-Me – I-Know it Now
About-Time – I'm-Finally-Doing
What-I've-Been – Needing to Do

(Chorus)
It Took A Long Time
I Had To Live Through Hell
Not Knowing What Love Could Do
'Til I Stopped Hating Myself And
Let Love Come Flowing Into My Heart

339. If You Say Yes Sexy Lady

Way-You-Walk – Really-Blows-My-Mind
Wow-Just as Nice – When-You-Turn-Around
Hey-Sexy – Can-I-Have a Moment of Your-Time
Don't-Get-Mad – When-I-Tell-You-This

You've-Got-The-Face – You've-Got-The-Ass
Sexy-Lady – Sexy-Lady – Why-Don't-You
Show-Me-The Rest of Your-Sexy-Body
Let's-Go-Spend-Some-Time – At-My-Place

(Chorus)
I Like Sex – How About You
You're Really Hot Looking
If You Say Yes Sexy Lady
We Can Do It Right Now
If You Say Yes Sexy Lady
We Can Do It Twice
If You Say Yes Sexy Lady
We Can Do It As Much As You Want To

If-You're-Having-Trouble – Talking and Moving
Sexy-Lady – Just-Blink a Few-Times
Letting-Me-Know – When-You're-Ready-For-More
Tell-Me-Sexy-Lady – How-Does it Feel
To be Counted as One of The-Blessed-Now

I-Know – That-I-Give it So-Fine
That-I – Really-Blew-Your-Mind
So go Ahead – Take-Your-Time
We-Have-All-Night – Sexy-Lady
You-Might-Want-To – Get-Up a Little-Slow
Looks-Like-My-Loving – Made-You-Kinda-Dizzy

(Chorus)
I Like Sex – How About You
You're Really Hot Looking
If You Say Yes Sexy Lady
We Can Do It Right Now
If You Say Yes Sexy Lady
We Can Do It Twice
If You Say Yes Sexy Lady
We Can Do It As Much As You Want To

340. Re-Grow My Love

I'm-Not a Bad-Person – I'm-Not a Great-Person
I-Am-Who-I-Am – Take-Me or Leave-Me
Just-Living-My-Life – The-Best-I-Can
Love-Being-Alive – But-Life
Is-Not-Being – Too-Kind
I'm-Tired of Being-Down
I'm-Not-Gonna – Take-It-Anymore

(Chorus)
Going To Get Ready To
Re-Grow My Love
I Feel It's Been Dead
For Far Too Long Now
And I Need To Feel Its Beauty Again

Going to Do-Something – Special
Going to Bring-Love – Back-Into-My-Heart
What do I-Have to Lose – Some-Passing-Time
That-Sucks – Hell-With-It – Darkness be Gone
Look at Me – I'm-Doing it Everybody
I'm-Freaking-Glowing – Wow-What a Trip
Who-Knew-Love – Could-Be-So-Powerful and True

(Chorus)
Going To Get Ready To
Re-Grow My Love
I Feel It's Been Dead
For Far Too Long Now
And I Need To Feel Its Beauty Again

Give-Me a Call if You're-Love-Blocked
I'll-Tell-You – My-Story of Sadness and Love
Might-Not-Be-For-You but You-Will-Feel
My-Pain-Of a Life – Before a Love – That-Morphed
Into-The-Loving-Life – Man-That-I've-Become

(Chorus)
Going To Get Ready To
Re-Grow My Love
I Feel It's Been Dead
For Far Too Long Now
And I Need To Feel Its Beauty Again

Come On All You Sex Having People

What is Love-Really – Compared to Hot-Sex
Love-May-Make – The-World-Go-Around
However-Sex-Makes-It – Go-Up-And-Down
Together-My-Sex – Having-Friends
We-Can – Change-The-World
With-Just-Humping and Moaning
What-Do-You – Say-World
Sounds-Like a Great-Time to Me

(Chorus)
Come On All You Sex Having People
Let's Have Sex Together Forever
Let's Stay Far Away From All The
Not Wanting To Have Sex People
And Keep On Getting It On And On

Clothes-Are-For – The-Wicked
And-All-The – Highly-Uptight
Or-Those-That-Think – Sex-Is a Sin
Don't-They-Know – It's-Our-World-Too
Time to Stand-Up-Proud – Together
With-All-Our – Clothes-Off
Showing-Off – What-Mother-Earth
Designed-From – Out of Her so Proudly

(Chorus)
Come On All You Sex Having People
Let's Have Sex Together Forever
Let's Stay Far Away From All The
Not Wanting To Have Sex People
And Keep On Getting It On And On

It-Makes-Me so Sad and Soft-Inside
That-All-The-Beautiful-People – Out-There
That-Want to Be – Truly-Free and Naked
Will-Never-Get to Be-Free-Enough
To-Show-The-World – What-They-Have
While-They-Are – Getting-It-On and On

(Repeat Chorus)

(Bonus Song)

A Sin A Day (Around The Corner Of Sex)

She-Smiles at You – Just-Don't-Smile-Back
Have to Be The-Man of Sex-Action
With-No-Time – For-Wasting
She's-Really-Hot and Built
Great-Thing – There's-Always a New-One
Just-Waiting to Be-Your-Next
Around-The-Corner of Sex

(Chorus #1)
A Sin A Day – Around The Corner Of Sex
Helps Keep A Good Man From Going Bad
When The World Keeps On Telling Him To Be
A Sin A Day – Around The Corner Of Sex
Helps Keep A Good Man From Going Bad
When The World Keeps On Telling Him To Be

Sex-Is-Not-Evil – It-Helps-Pass-Time
Especially – When-You-Don't
Have a Lot to Say to The-Person
That-You – Just-Want to Have-Sex-With

(Chorus #1)
A Sin A Day – Around The Corner Of Sex
Helps Keep A Good Man From Going Bad
When The World Keeps On Telling Him To Be
A Sin A Day – Around The Corner Of Sex
Helps Keep A Good Man From Going Bad
When The World Keeps On Telling Him To Be

Time-Ticks-Away – A-Man – Is-At-His-Best
When-He – Is-Having-Sex
Just-Let-Him-Be – As-He-Feels-No-Sin
Only-Sex-That-Makes – The-World-Go-Up and Down

(Chorus #2)
A Sin A Day – Around The Corner Of Sex
Helps Keep A Good Man From Going Bad
When The World Keeps On Telling Him To Be
A Sin A Day – Around The Corner Of Sex
Is Alot Better Than Pain And Death

F.M.L. (Freeze My Love)

Winter-Time – I-Will-Not-Let-You – Freeze-My-Love
Pains of The-World – Coming at Me – I-Feel so Isolated
Being-Left Alone to Understand – What-I-Cannot-Change

Winter-Time – I-Will-Not-Let-You – Freeze-My-Love
You're a Giant – I'm-But a Man – That-Never-Surrenders
Send-Forth-Your-Arctic-Blast – I'll-Feel a Summer's-Breeze

Winter-Time – I-Will-Not-Let-You – Freeze-My-Love
Come to Me as Furious as You-Will – I'll-Survive
I am Alive – You are But a Season

Winter-Time – I-Will-Not-Let-You – Freeze-My-Love
There is Someone-Out-There – Fighting-Your-Bitterness
Thinking-About-Someone – Just-Like-Me

Winter-Time – I-Will-Not-Let-You – Freeze-My-Love
One-Day – I-Will Find so Soft – Of-Flesh to Press-Against
That-Our-Body-Heat-Together – Will-Melt-You – All-Away

L.K.G. (Last Kiss Goodbye)

It's-Time Baby – I-Gotta be Going – It's-Time
For-Our – Last-Kiss-Goodbye – Wish-I had More-Time
But so Sad – My-Time is Here – My-Final-Sleep

Quick-Quick – Kiss-Me-Darling – You're-Fading-Away
It's-Time – For-Our – Last-Kiss-Goodbye
Who is – What is That in The-Corner – It's-Staring at Me

If-You-Want-Our – Last-Kiss-Goodbye – It's-Now or Never
My-Death's a Lady – A-Very-Fine and Naked-Lady
Heaven-Help-Me – She is Licking-Her-Lips and Shaking-Her-Tail

Our-Last-Kiss-Goodbye – On-My-Lips – As-I-Cross-Over
No-Pain – No-Fear – Lady of Death is So-Fine
But-She is One-Big-Tease – Laughing at Me – Leading-Me
To the Gates of Hell – My-Crime for Being a Very-Big-Cheater
At-Least-I-Get to Remember – Our-Last-Kiss-Goodbye – Still
I'd-Rather be Alive and Getting-Laid – Peace and Love to You

Story Four: Sadie And The Man

"Wow!" "Wow, that's your pick up?"

"I don't know hottie, Wow says it all. You look so fine, you're dressed to be totally sexy, your face, your hair, you look so fine everywhere. In my mind I have a mental picture of what I always wanted and beautiful you are the closet to perfection my eyes have ever seen. Sorry I was overwhelmed and instantly got turned on. Rude of me in such a place like this. But sexy eyes how can I put this without the chance of you walking away for me?"

"Just be cool and hot and give me a kiss." "With tongue?" "No, no tongue yet. Be patient I will tell you when it is time to use your tongue."

"Oh yes tell me when darling and do not forget to tell me when I can bite you so soft and sexy on your sweet fine looking ass."

Lady looks at man and says with a smile on her lips like you horny bastard and says, "My tonight, you can do that right now." "Now?" "Yes. Now don't stand there come over here and bite me on my ass really nice and sexy. Who knows if you do a great job I might even turn around and let you, well all I can say is you better know more than enough not to bite me there. You do, don't you?"

"Yes I do and I can proudly add this, I am marvelous at both the front and rear so rest assured I'm happy to be your tonight and as hot as I am right now you will be just as hot and burning with passion. I'll give you my few licks and many pulsations promise. You, my fantasy will moan free and full in ecstasy before I have my full level of ecstasy released."

"Are you married? What is your name?" "No I am single and just call me Man and I will call you Lady. Let us find out tomorrow morning if we want to become real people to each other."

"Damn Man you have me wanting to make love to you right here in front of everybody." "Sounds hot but there will be a let down if we did." "What is that?"

"We would not be finished before some rude person told us to stop doing what we are doing." "You are a smart man I'll give you that."

"Now here comes some doom and gloom for you Man." "What kinda of doom and gloom?"

"My date just showed up, I see him walking in the door now. He looks pissed, oh what will you do?"

"Well my tonight, and maybe tomorrow once again, if there is a front door there is a back door so let's get going so we can have the sexual time of our lives. What do you say Lady? Stay and have the same and maybe even find yourself some normal love on down the line. Which would be a very big shame for I offer you just hot passion with a who knows if there will ever be love. Will you stay with I love you man or come with me and get screwed like you have never experienced before?"

"Okay Man let's go screw, you better do more than just rock my world, because my man that is coming to us faster is getting serious with me. And you want to know the hottest thing?"

"Yes I do." "I have not made love to him yet and tonight was going to be the first time." "Lady I love you." "I love you too Man, let's go."

Lady and Man run away hearing the pleas of her man saying, "Please Sadie don't do this to me, I love you. Who is that bastard that you are leaving with? He looks like a sorry bastard that will only use you. Can you hear me Sadie? I love you, please come back to me, I'll forgive you for your mistake of acting like a slut."

Sadie stops running and says, "Slut. This coming from a man that has not had me yet."

Everybody within ear shot listens and watches as Sadie is about to let loose with all the mixed up feelings she has had inside her for the past six months since she has been dating Barney.

"And you want to know why that is Barney? Don't answer cause I am going to tell you whether you want to know or not. You don't turn me on. Sure you're a good man but I need a real man, a man that will turn me on."

Barney all shook up says, "But you promised that I could finally have you. I have waited six long months for you to get over your last boyfriend.

You said you wanted a non-sexual relationship until you felt comfortable enough to make love again."

"Well Barney that was what I wanted, someone to be there as a friend giving me friendship and companionship until, hee, hee." "Until what Sadie?"

"Until my man came back to me tonight promising me what I have been missing from him for the past six months." "This is him the one that cheated on you with everyone you knew?"

"Yes the one and only. Before you think you still have a chance remember what you look like and look at him. He is so fine I am love putty in his hands."

"How can you do this to me Sadie?" "Easy when I am not with my man I am a heart breaker to all those that try to sway me from my one and only." (Silence.)

"I can't believe this, I loved you." "You don't still love me Barney?" "Yes I do. Yes I do. Will you come back to me now?" "Let me think. No I will not you loser." "Loser? Better a loser than a slut."

"That's enough ass face, fun time is over, one more word and I'll whip your ass . Now run off and go whack off, you pathetic, sorry piece of crap."

Barney has no luck tonight as he runs at Man not seeing the glass on the floor three feet in front of him. Barney steps on the glass at full speed and slips off it, sending him tripping through five tables before he finally falls on the floor, knocked out.

"Should I take his wallet Man?" "No Sadie leave it we do not need it." "We don't?" "Nope not anymore, I finally hit the big score baby we're set for life." "You promise this time is it? No more scheming and waiting?"

"That's right baby my pretty, pretty Sadie, the old hag has died. In just a few days I will be a very, very rich and single man. And Sadie I want you by my side in my time of grief and of course underneath me and on top of me."

"Of course my man I am all yours to do as you may."

"I am so looking forward to that Sadie. Six months and you never once had sex?" "Nope not even once." "Wow Sadie you are going to feel incredible." "No Man, I am going to feel like perfection".

Sadie and Man leave the club and go to Man's mansion and make love from nine o'clock pm until two am. Three days later they both go to the funeral of Man's late wife both wearing black. Sadie wore a very short, hot and sexy looking dress that made every man and even some of the women at the funeral want to have her right there beside the coffin. Man with no tears in his eyes rubbed Sadie's long sexy legs all the way up 'til he had her moaning and asking for more.

Five days have gone by, two days since Man's wife has been buried and it is time to find out how rich Man is to become. In a lawyer's office Man and Sadie sit together separated from the rest of his late wife's family. A family that hates him so very much that he is known to them as the horrible bastard that took advantage of their sister, their mother, their grandmother and so on. In other words they all feel like they deserve all the money and Man deserves nothing. Man smiles as he rubs his eye with his middle finger. Then all is silent as Mr. Lawyer walks in.

"Hello everybody. I hope all that are suppose to be here are present?"

No one answers until Man says, "I'm here and that's all that matters."

"Very good then," Mr. Lawyer says, "Let's move this along shall we?" Silence once again. "I have to tell you that this is the easiest will I have ever had to read. Mrs. Judy Morton wants me to inform every one here that not one of you are to receive anything. All holdings, all her money, everything she has left behind is to go to different charities. Well that's it. Good day everybody and good fortune to you."

The office erupts in shouts of anger including Man who is shouting the loudest that he had to have sex with that old hag and this is not right.

Sadie gets out of her seat with tears in her eyes then she finds Barney and marries him living every day happily telling him what to do and how to do it. Man is trying to find another old woman to marry.

(Bonus 7 Inch)
No-No-No – Baby (155.)
(Side – **A**) / (Written: 08-??-2013)
Hips A Rockin' (71.)
(Side – **B**) / (Written: 06-??-2013)

No-No-No – Baby (155.)

I-Asked – You-Said-Yes
Next-Night – I-Asked-Your-Friend
She-Said – Yes-Yes-Yes
She-Was-Good – You-Were-Great

Next-Night – We're at It-Again
You-Tell-Me – That-You-Love-Me
I-Pretend – That-I'm-Sleeping
Sex is Fine – Love is Something-Else
Knock-Knock – Your-Friend – My-Last-Night
Come a Knocking – I-Guess – I-Better-Tell-The-Truth

(Chorus)
No-No-No – Baby
I Did Not Have Sex With Her
She Is Lying – She Is Jealous
Trying To Make You Hate Me
Because I Told Her – No-No-No

No-Cat-Fight – Just-Me – Out and Gone
Best-Friends-Forever – Don't-Share
Friend-That-Was-Good – Still-Jealous
Willing to Become – Great-For-Me

Then-One-Night – Third-Friend – Why-Not-Once
Once-Was-The-Best so Far – Then-Came a Knock-Knock
Friend's-Yelling – I'm-Naked – Ready-For-Loving
I-Guess – I-Better – Tell the Truth

(Chorus)
No-No-No – Baby
I Did Not Have Sex With Her
She Is Lying – She Is Jealous
Trying To Make You Hate Me
Because I Told Her – No-No-No

90

Hips A Rockin' (71.)

(She)
Baby-That's-It – Nibble-On-My-Ear
Love-Me – Slow-And-Easy
Give-My – Honey-Sweet-Lips
Kisses – That-Make-Me-Shiver
Let-Me – Feel-The-Red – Rose of Love

(He)
Baby-Give-Me – That-Hungry-Stare
Make-My-Body – Hard in Delight
I-Want to Be – Hot-With-Desire
Don't-Stop – Don't-You-Dare
Take-Your-Time – We're-Just-Starting

(Chorus) (Both)
When We Get Our Hips A Rockin'
Hot Rockin' Loving Fills The Air
When We Get Our Hips A Rockin'
Nobody Better Come A Knockin'
When We Get Our Hips A Rockin'
The World Can Go Rock Itself

(Her)
Caress-My-Heart – Allow-Me to Catch – My-Breath
I'm-Losing – My-Mind – I-Know-The-Deal
You're a Lover – Not an I-Love-You
Will-You be Back – Is-This-Goodbye
Why-Can't-Love – Be as Simple as Lust

(He)
Luscious-Talk-Later – Can't-Think-Right-Now
Overdrive – My-Body is In-Overdrive – Love is Not-Around
Lust is Fueling-Me – Catch-Your-Breath – After-We're-Done
Don't-Worry-Baby – I'll be Back – Very-Soon

(Chorus) (Both)
When We Get Our Hips A Rockin'
Hot Rockin' Loving Fills The Air
When We Get Our Hips A Rockin'
Nobody Better Come A Knockin'
When We Get Our Hips A Rockin'
The World Can Go Rock Itself

Contest Number One
(Peace, Freedom, Singing And A Pause)
(AKA: A Pause – A Singing Contest)
(Pages 92-99)

Are You Ready (Today Is The Day) (696.) **(Group)**

Can We Rise Beyond Ourselves (697.) **(Group)**

Tickle Your Heart (694.) **(Contestant #1)**

Love Is Everywhere (695.) **(Contestant #2)**

Good Night (698.) **(Group)**

In this book lies something special that I want to see come to life. It is five songs designed for a singing contest. Three group songs and two separate contestant songs. The show starts with everybody that is a contestant on stage preforming

Are You Ready (Today Is The Day)

Are-You-Ready – To-Have a Great-Time
Are-You-Ready – For-Something-Different
Are-You-Ready – Clap-Your-Hands
Feel-This – In-Your-Hearts
Today is The-Day – We-All-Take a Pause – Together
Today is The Day – We-Will-Embrace – Difference
Today is The-Day – We-Show the World
That-Different – Can-Get-Along

Great message that is not only for the contestant but also for the audience members as well. Nobody showing up to complain about what's going on in the world. Just people showing up on a day they all decide for themselves to leave all their heavy at the gates. Some would say to me that this is a lot for me or anyone else to ask of people. I do not see this that way. I do not want anybody to show up feeling like they have to do this because it is the thing to do at this point in time. This show is a show for different people getting together to prove that it can be done. That is only part of it, the other part lies solely on every individual that shows up. They are showing up not only for the world to take notice of but they are also showing up for themselves.

This world can make your inner self feel like it's been beaten down. Some have become harsh to life, it is hard to smile longer than a few seconds at a time. Looking at strangers that are different than them as warning signs of danger. Nothing can change the world in one day, all that show up will know that outside the gates of this show will be people that like them and dislike them for who they are. Here is the great thing about this show, everyone that comes to this show will be there for themselves to embrace difference. Thousands of people with their eyes open noticing things they have not noticed before for fear will be weak inside the gates of this show.

Barriers will be broken down as enlightenment blossoms slowly to the realization that change can become a reality no matter what the rest of the world deems as impossible or unattainable. One Day, One Pause together is all I'm asking.

93

I would love to be in a place that is filled up with thousands of different kinds of people that do not want to hurt me or anyone else there. Wow maybe I'm asking too much but "Love It" I do not care. If somebody wants to hate me for this, be my guest and I'll just ignore you. Everybody can bleed I am no different. Everybody can make someone else bleed it is so very easy. We been there, we done that, Humanity is brutal. This is not a secret, Humanity is also loving. We have come so very far my Mind Rockers. Tomorrow's dream of love and peace in a peaceful world cannot be obtained by force nor can it be obtained when hate and fear is allowed to be present out of a obligation of compassion. The only thing that truly will stop someone from coming to this show will be themselves.

Call me a dreamer, tell me that I dwell in some fantasy reality where everything is nothing but La,La,La,La,La. I will tell you there are walls that I cannot climb over by myself. Yet in these walls are holes that I can see through to the other side of enlightenment. Yes I am selfish, I want to get to the other side of these walls. I would love this but what good would it do me if I climbed and climbed and dug my nails in deeper and deeper as I ascended to the top and when I finally got to the other side I was all by myself? Is that not where I am right now? Is this not why I'm am trying to climb over these walls?

I guess world watch me climb by myself as I get higher and higher or climb up this first wall right beside me. This is not about your family, This is not about your friends. This is not about your country or the world. This is about you and what you want inside yourself first. Then comes the hard part made easier and easier every day as our numbers spread across the world. We will be We because we will all have ascended to a higher plane of thinking. They will be they because of fear and hate.

Nothing positive will ever grow out of fear and hate unless you count death. Let Mr. Death do his counting and mark his marks, We will be too busy living our new lives to their fullest. Until the day comes that there will be no more rich and no more poor. When We will not need powerful governments anymore to start the next war. The next war might be the very last one Mother Earth can stand, for We are her guests no matter how powerful We become.

Peace and Love to You Mind Rockers.

The Gemini Rising Rockin' Machine

Are You Ready (Today Is The Day) (696.)
(Contestant Group Song) (Written 01/28/2015)

Are-You-Ready – To-Have a Great-Time
Are-You-Ready – For-Something-Different

Are-You-Ready – Clap-Your-Hands
Feel-This – In-Your-Hearts

Today is The-Day – We-All-Take a Pause- – Together
Today is The-Day – We-Will-Embrace – Difference

Today is The-Day – We-Show-The-World
That-Different – Can-Get-Along

Today is The-Day – We-Prove-What-Tomorrow
Can-Be-Like – For-Everyone in This-World

La, La, La, La, La, La, La, La, La, La
La, La, La, La, La, La, La, La, La, La
La, La, La, La, La, La, La, La, La, La

Are-You-Ready – To-Have a Great-Time
Are-You-Ready – For-Something-Different

Are-You-Ready – Clap-Your-Hands
Feel-This – In-Your-Hearts

Today is The-Day – We-All-Take a Pause – Together
Today is The-Day – We-Will-Embrace – Difference

Today is The-Day – We-Show-The-World
That-Different – Can-Get-Along

Today is The-Day – We-Prove-What-Tomorrow
Can-Be-Like – For-Everyone in This-World

La, La, La, La, La, La, La, La, La, La
La, La, La, La, La, La, La, La, La, La
La, La, La, La, La, La, La, La, La, La

Can We Rise Beyond Ourselves (697.)
(Contestant Group Song) (Written 01/28/2015)

We-Are-Alone – We-Are-Lonely
No-One-Knows – Who-We-Are
Which-Is-Sad – For-We-Are-Special
We-Are-Scarred – We-Are-Battered
No-One-Knows – Who-We-Are
Which-Is-Sad – For-We-Are-Special

We-Like to Understand – Life-More
Embrace as Many – Cultures as We-Can
No-One-Knows – Who-We-Are
Today is The-Day – That-Changes

(Chorus)
Can We Rise Beyond Ourselves
Yes We Can – We Can Feel It
Can We Rise Beyond Ourselves
Yes We Can – We Will Rise Beyond
Can We Rise Beyond Ourselves
Yes We Can – To Help Humanity
Can We Rise Beyond Ourselves
Yes We Can – To Change The World – And This
Starts Today – With We – And All Of You

Welcome to The-Show – We-Hope
That-You're-Enjoying – Your-Pause
For-The-Day – We-Thank-You
And-Hope – You-Take-With-You-This
Everyone is Different – And-That's-Okay
Please-Sing – Along-With-Us

(Chorus)
Can We Rise Beyond Ourselves
Yes We Can – We Can Feel It
Can We Rise Beyond Ourselves
Yes We Can – We Will Rise Beyond
Can We Rise Beyond Ourselves
Yes We Can – To Help Humanity
Can We Rise Beyond Ourselves
Yes We Can – To Change The World – And This
Starts Today – With We – And All Of You

Tickle Your Heart (694.)
(Contestant Solo Song #1) (Written 01/27/2015)

Do-You – See-Me
Do-You-Know – Who-I-Am
I-Am a Fancier of Love
That-Feels in You a Lost-Love

A-Love-That-Needs to Be-Rekindled
By-Someone – That is Full of Love
Touch-Me – Feel-Me – I'm-Real
Just-Let-Loose – Your-Fears – and

(Chorus)
Let Me Tickle Your Heart
With My Love
Let Me Tickle Your Heart
With My Love
Let Me Tickle Your Heart
With My Love
Let Me Show You A Love
That Will Tickle Your Heart

Warm-Lover – You're-Almost-Hot
It's so Hard-For-You to Believe in Love
I-Understand – Your-Heart
Has-Been-Broken – Many-Times

Lover – That-Was-Them – Not-I
I-Love-You – Trust in My-Love
One-More-Step and You'll be Free
Free to Be in Love – With-Me
Without-Ever – Having to Worry
If-I – Still-Love-You

(Chorus)
Let Me – Tickle Your Heart
With My Love
Let Me – Tickle Your Heart
With My Love
Let Me – Tickle Your Heart
With My Love
Let Me Show You A Love
That Will Tickle Your Heart
97

Love Is Everywhere (695.)
(Contestant Solo Song #2) (Written 01/27/2015)

Four-Steps – Back-Too-Far
Two-Hearts – Never-Meet
Just-Another – Lost-Love
That-Was Meant to Be
Gone-Forever – Out of Sight

Sunshine and Waterfalls
Moon-Beams and Ice-Cream
Love is Everywhere
As a Balance to Loneliness

(Chorus)
Love Is Everywhere
Everywhere Is Love
On This Beautiful World
Just Open Your Eyes – Believe
Watch It Appear To You Like
It's Never Been There Before

Love is Forever – Forever is Love
Now-You-See-It – Now-It's-There
Everywhere to Feel
Like a Lost – Forgotten-Dream

Sadness – Brings-You-Pain – Your-Heart
Pounds-Out-Your-Misery – For a Past-Life
Not-Fulfilled – With-Love

Darkness-Begins to Fade-Away
Replaced – Forever by Love
A-Love – That-Will be With-You
Until-You-Fly – High in The-Sky

(Chorus)
Love Is Everywhere
Everywhere Is Love
On This Beautiful World
Just Open Your Eyes – Believe
Watch It Appear To You Like
It's Never Been There Before

Good Night (698.)
(Contestant Group Song) (Written 01/28/2015)

We-Hope-You – Had a Great-Time
On Such a Beautiful – Sunny-Day
We-Wish – We-Could do This – Again
Tomorrow-And-The-Day – After-That
And-The-Day – After-That

(Chorus)
Good Night Everybody
Everybody Good Night
It's Time To Find Out
Who The Winners Is
Good Night Everybody
Everybody Good Night
Thank You For Your Pause
Thank You For Your Vote

Good Night Everybody
Everybody Good Night
Good Night Everybody
Good Night To You

We-Hope-You – Had a Great-Time
On Such a Beautiful – Sunny-Day
We-Wish – We-Could do This – Again
Tomorrow-And-The-Day – After-That
And-The-Day – After-That

(Chorus)
Good Night Everybody
Everybody Good Night
It's Time To Find Out
Who The Winners Is
Good Night Everybody
Everybody Good Night
Thank You For Your Pause
Thank You For Your Vote

Good Night Everybody
Everybody Good Night
Good Night Everybody
Good Night To You
99

Contest Number Two
(Let's Turn The World On)
(Pages 100-105)
(Written September 06/07 2016)

Let's Party (956.)

Save The World (957.)

Love Not Nuclear Weapons (958.)

Let's Turn The World On (959.)

The Two Song Ending: (960.)
I. The World At War
II. What A Shame (I'm Dead And Gone)

Let's Party (956.)

Heaven and Hell
The-Right and The-Left
The-Opposites – That-Don't Attract
Causing-The-World to Suck

I-Have a Heart – I-Have a Mind
I-Want-Peace – Not-Endless-Crap
I'm-Not a Fish – Out of Water
Don't-Have an Extra-Hole
In-My-Head – That-Makes-Me-Gullible

(Chorus)
Let's Party – Let's Party Tonight
All The Powerful Countries
Are A Bunch Of Hoarders
Of Yesterdays Horrors
Let's Party – Let's Party Tonight
Then Tomorrow – When We're Sober
Let's Take Over The World
Before It Becomes Quite Clear
That There's No More Reason To Party

Old-Spoiled-Brats
That-Are – Lousy in The-Sack
Make-All-The-Decisions
That-Makes – This-World-Bleed

I-Am-Me – You-Are-You
They-Are-They – They-Will-Never-Change
I-Don't-Care-Anymore – How-About-You

(Chorus)
Let's Party – Let's Party Tonight
All The Powerful Countries
Are A Bunch Of Hoarders
Of Yesterdays Horrors
Let's Party – Let's Party Tonight
Then Tomorrow – When We're Sober
Let's Take Over The World
Before It Becomes Quite Clear
That There's No More Reason To Party

101

Save The World (957.)

While-I'm-Enjoying
Your-Love-Slice
While-Your-Enjoying
My-Long – Love-Bone
I'm-Just a Wondering
Do-You-Love – The-World
As-Much as You – Enjoy-Sex

Not-Trying To Be-Heavy
Just-Taking a Break
Don't-Worry – Our-Loving-Will
Continue-Forth – Extra-Fine and Wild

(Chorus)
After We're Finished Making Love
I Think I Want To Save The World
I Feel Great Right Now Baby
But After We're Done – I'll Be Bummed
Because The World's Filled With Killers
That Rather Kill Than Get Laid
Think About That Baby – Then Join Me
On My Way To Save The World

Let-Me-Lay-Down – Wow-What-Loving
Baby-You're-Fine – Hang-On
Let's-Think-About-This – For a Moment
Okay-I-Got-It – Let's-Stay-Naked

Two – Maybe-Three – Hours-More
That-Should – Hold-Back – For-Awhile
My-Urge to Enjoy – Your-Fine-Body
That-Makes-Me – Love-The-World

(Chorus)
After We're Finished Making Love
I Think I Want To Save The World
I Feel Great Right Now Baby
But After We're Done – I'll Be Bummed
Because The World's Filled With Killers
That Rather Kill Than Get Laid
Think About That Baby – Then Join Me
On My Way To Save The World

Love Not Nuclear Weapons (958.)

Nuclear-Weapons – They-Suck – Humanity
All-The-Animals – All-The-Mountains
All-The-Oceans – They-Don't-Stand a Chance

Why-Do-We – Still-Have-Them
Why-Do-We – Still-Allow-Them
Nuclear-Weapons – They-Suck
They're-Not-Needed – Anymore
Were-They – Ever-Needed
I-Say-No – I-Say-No-Way

(Chorus)
Love Not Nuclear Weapons
Will Save The World
Don't You Understand
Nuclear Weapons Suck
They Can Destroy The World
Love Not Nuclear Weapons
Will Save The World
Don't You Understand
All It Takes Is One Crazy Person
To Destroy The World

Nuclear-Weapons – They-Suck
Why-Do-We – Still-Have-Them
Why-Do-We – Still-Allow-Them
Nuclear-Weapons – They-Suck
They're-Not-Needed – Anymore
Were-They – Ever-Needed
I-Say-No – I-Say-No-Way

(Chorus)
Love Not Nuclear Weapons
Will Save The World
Don't You Understand
Nuclear Weapons Suck
They Can Destroy The World
Love Not Nuclear Weapons
Will Save The World
Don't You Understand
All It Takes Is One Crazy Person
To Destroy The World

Let's Turn The World On (959.)

I-Have-Sixty-Nine – Dollars in My-Pocket
Not-Much – That's-True – I-Know
In-My-Soul – I'm-Hungry and Sober
I-Can-Smile – At-Least-I'm-Not-Broke
I-Have-Enough – For a Cheap-Room
To-Get-Laid – All-Night-Long

What Do You Say Baby
Would You Like To Get Laid
I'm Willing And Able
To Share My Room With You

(Chorus)
Baby Let's Turn The World On
I'm Turned On – You're Turned On
Let's Go Get Laid Right Now
Baby I Know It's A Big Responsibility
Let's Get Laid So Great And Giant
That We'll Turn The World On
Before All The Bad Destroys It

I-Have-Sixty-Nine – Dollars in My-Pocket
Not-Much – That's-True – I-Know
In-My-Soul – I'm-Hungry and Sober
I-Can-Smile – At-Least-I'm-Not-Broke
I-Have-Enough – For a Cheap-Room
To-Get-Laid – All-Night-Long

What Do You Say Baby
Would You Like To Get Laid
I'm Willing And Able
To Share My Room With You

(Chorus)
Baby Let's Turn The World On
I'm Turned On – You're Turned On
Let's Go Get Laid Right Now
Baby I Know It's A Big Responsibility
Let's Get Laid So Great And Giant
That We'll Turn The World On
Before All The Bad Destroys It

The Two Song Ending: (960.)
I. The World At War
II. What A Shame (I'm Dead And Gone)

I. The World At War

Sunny-Day in July
It-Was-Hot – It-Was-Beautiful
Life-Was-Great – Life-Was-Miserable
There-Was-War – But-No-World-War

One-Bomb – Two-Bombs – One-Hundred-Bombs
The-World-Was at War – Stupid-Humans
The-World-War – Lasted-Just-One-Day
I-Was-Eating-Lunch – When-I-Died at 12:33

(Chorus)
The World At War
What A Stupid Concept
The World At War
Mostly Bombs – Hardly Any Bullets
The World At War
One Moment Mother Earth Was Fine
The Next Moment – She Was Cracked In Half

II. What A Shame (I'm Dead And Gone)

I-Was-Alive so Was-Mother-Earth
I'm a Ghost – I'm a Spirit
I'm-Something – From-The-Other-Side
It's-Hard to Understand – I'm-Alone

I'm-Watching-Somehow – The-Earth-Burn
It's-Not a Pretty-Sight – I-Can't-Cry
I-Have-No-Eyes – Mouth or Nose
Such a Strange-Afterlife – I'm-Living

(Chorus)
What A Shame – I'm Dead And Gone
What A Shame – My Afterlife Sucks
What A Shame – I'm Dead And Gone
What A Shame – My Afterlife Sucks
What A Shame – I'm Dead And Gone
What A Shame – My Afterlife Sucks

www.ingramcontent.com/pod-product-compliance
Lightning Source LLC
Chambersburg PA
CBHW070505130626
46555CB00003B/1167